reaching
DUSTIN

reaching DUSTIN

vicki grove

SCHOLASTIC INC.

New York Toronto London Auckland Sydney
Mexico City New Delhi Hong Kong

ISBN 0-439-13403-X

12 11 10 9 8 7 6 5 4 3 2 1   9/9 0 1 2 3 4/0

Printed in the U.S.A.   40

First Scholastic printing, November 1999

Book design by Gunta Alexander. Text set in Baskerville.

I spent part of the summer between third and fourth grade at the home of my aunt Maxine. My favorite pastime those muggy July afternoons was to disappear beneath her big kitchen table with a book and some pots and pans. From there in my teepee I would read aloud and loudly, accompanying myself on tom-toms. Meanwhile, my audience, Aunt Maxine, prepared dinner in that steamy kitchen for a houseful of sweaty kids.

Any normal person would have suggested I go outside and read to Bowser, the family dog. Aunt Maxine, though, has never been a normal person. "Vicki," I remember her saying, two or three times each performance, "you are a very good reader."

For this and a thousand other gifts of spirit, this book is dedicated to my wonderful teacher aunt, Maxine Baum Erkiletian.

reaching DUSTIN

one

I got *you*," I croaked to the top of Dustin Groat's bent head. My heart was beating in this raggedy way, and my stomach felt . . . bouncy. *Calm down, Carly!* I ordered myself.

Dustin didn't look at me. He just scrinched his left ear against his shoulder. Was he trying to signal that he wasn't even going to listen? Before I could chicken out, I crouched down and got right in his face.

"I said, I got *you*. I drew *your* name! To interview!"

As usual, Dustin was slumped in his chair, staring at his desk in this way that made you wonder if he was actually asleep with his eyes open. His arms were stretched across a white skull and crossbones on a faded gray T-shirt. The words *Harley Davidson* showed just below them, and a black motorcycle took a bumpy ride over his skinny rib cage. The sweat-stained leather band he always wore across his forehead pushed his grease-spiked hair into unplanned-looking directions, and there was a pool of cloddy mud where his heavy black boots had shed all over the floor.

In fact, a thin trail of that cloddy mud connected his shoved-into-the corner desk to the rectangle of lined-up desks used by all of us regular people in Ms. Aspen's sixth-grade class. There wasn't even a desk nearby for me to sit at to interview him.

Dustin slowly took his hands from his armpits and began picking at a safety pin he had stuck through the crusty skin on the back of one of his knuckles. His light eyes flickered toward me through long, spidery lashes. Then he looked listlessly down at the floor and dropped one arm to scoop up a pencil that was lying in his boot dirt. He stuck the point of that filthy pencil into the ear he'd been scrinching.

"Don't!" It took all my control not to grab his wrist and pull his hand away. "You'll puncture your eardrum!"

He closed his eyes and stuck his hands into his armpits again, leaving the pencil poking out of his ear like an arrow shot into his brain.

"Who cares?" he mumbled.

At lunch, Randi and Alicia thought the fact that I'd drawn Dustin for our interview project was just hilarious.

"He's so, like, totally obnoxious!" Randi blurted out, shaking her waist-length hair away from her shoulders. "Ask him why he head butts the girls on the slide ladder, Carly. Or why he cusses. Or, wait—I know!" She picked up her corn dog and held it like a microphone under Ali's nose. "Pardon me, Mr. Groat, but how often do you smoke that marijuana your family grows?"

Ali and I laughed, of course, but I sneaked a look over my shoulder to see if any of the teachers patrolling the cafeteria had heard.

"I wouldn't exactly call him obnoxious, though," Alicia said, sliding the little acrobat charm back and forth along the chain of her necklace like she does when she's thinking hard about something. Her small face was tilted to the side, and her pale skin and tons of orange hair seemed to be glowing. Sometimes, especially when she's doing one of her gymnastics routines, Ali reminds me of a delicate fairy, lit from within. "I mean, he hasn't really head butted anyone since way back in, what? Miss Tyleson's class? And we don't even *use* the slide anymore. Obnoxious is loud, but Dustin is quiet now. He's more like . . ."

"Gross!" Randi pronounced. "He's *gross!*"

The boys at the table next to us glanced over when Randi squealed that last *gross*. But then, boys look over when Randi does anything, lately.

"Ask him how many tattoos he's got!" Randi bounced in her seat. "His dad and his uncles have so many you

3

can't see the skin on their arms!" She leaned forward and added in a loud whisper, "And some are of naked ladies!"

Again, Ali and I hunched our shoulders and giggled, but when we were through I thought about that for a second and pointed out, "But just because his uncles have them doesn't mean Dustin does. Who could tell? He always wears those long-sleeved motorcycle T-shirts, even when it's hot."

Ali nodded, agreeing. "Dustin's just a kid, like us. They may not get tattoos till they're older."

"Dustin's just a kid, Ali, but he is *not* like us," Randi insisted. She started snapping her fingers and flipping her hair, doing dance moves to a beat in her head. Probably she'd noticed that the boys were watching. "All the Groats live together in a creepy compound somewhere, not in regular separate houses like normal people. And they're always in and out of jail for drugs or fighting." She closed her eyes and swayed with the beat.

It's been a little hard to have a real conversation with Randi since she got her beloved satellite dish last August and started dancing along with rock videos non-stop. Still, we all knew that jail stuff was true because we all got the *Cooper's Glade Gazette* each Friday. Besides the comics and "Dear Abby," the police report was usually the only interesting part.

"Everybody's always talking about Dustin's dad and uncles and grown-up cousins, but I never hear anybody say anything about any girl Groats," I murmured.

4

"Does Dustin have a mother?" I kept thinking about the way Dustin had shoved that pencil into his ear. And what about that *pin* sticking out of his *hand?* Would any mother let you get away with that?

"Maybe they created Dustin in that drug lab everybody says they have!" Randi's eyes snapped open, wide with excitement. "Then they wouldn't need girls! Ask him that, Carly!"

"Shhhh, Randi!" Ali cautioned, stifling her laughter, and this time I wasn't the only one checking nervously for teachers.

I turned back around and quickly shoved my tray aside to make room for the writing notebook that I've carried with me all the time this year, slung over my shoulder on a yarn strap it took me forever to braid.

"Car-*lee!*" Randi protested as I flipped through to a new, clean page. "Don't *think* now! Please? It's *lunch!* You said you wouldn't *think* at lunch!"

I began, centering my title carefully: *Interview Questions.*

"You heard Ms. Aspen, Randi," I told her. "We just had to introduce ourselves to the person we drew today, but tomorrow we begin interviewing for real, then the person who turns in the most in-depth interview report two weeks from now gets to be editor of our sixth-grade newspaper. I *have* to get started thinking up good questions!"

Some of our other friends had just walked up and were putting their trays on our table.

"You'll get editor, Carly," Jasmine said, shrugging in this bored way as she sat down.

Alicia smiled at me in support and nodded along so hard her crinkly orange hair blurred through the air like an out-of-control blaze.

"You guys!" I whispered, flustered, hoping no one at the tables around us had heard. I *wanted* to be editor so much it hurt, but what if everybody *knew* how much I wanted it, and then I didn't *get* it?

"Who else *could* be editor, Carly?" Alicia asked in this quiet way she has that makes everyone instantly pay attention. "You won Mr. Farleigh's poetry contest last year," she said, ticking things off on her fingers. "You got the only *A* on our first sixth-grade-English essay. And everybody asks you when they need to know how to spell something because everybody knows you're the best writer."

Ali figures things out like she moves her feet along the balance beam, putting each thought carefully after the one before it. But just because she ends up with a precise and perfect line of reasons for something doesn't mean her predictions always come true.

"You'll get editor, and we'll be equal again!" Randi announced, swaying to a beat only she was hearing. "I'm class president, Ali's gymnastics-team captain, and you'll be editor. E-qual, E-qual, oh yeah, uh-huh, e-QUAL! Carl, you just need to have faith in yourself! Have FAITH, girl!"

Like I said, it's been hard to really talk to Randi

lately, especially when she's in her dance mode. I would have loved to point out that her being elected class president had nothing to do with faith and lots to do with the cute, flouncy skirts she was wearing and her outrageous attitude this year and waist-length swishy hair.

But even more, I would have liked to ask about something *else* she maybe didn't even realize she'd just said.

Since when were she and Ali and I not equal best friends?

two

At home that evening, we ate dinner outside on the picnic table, like we usually do in the fall. In late September the view from our farm is beautiful in all directions. The air was so clear that I could see a glare that was the roof of Randi's trailer a couple of miles off to the right. In fact, I could even see her satellite dish and the three long, bright-blue chicken barns behind it. Off to the left, on a hill even higher than ours and covered with red and orange trees, Alicia's three-story farmhouse perched like an abandoned white bride.

My seventeen-year-old brother, Noah, suddenly jabbed me in the ribs with his elbow as he reached for a second piece of apricot pie. "Sorry, Carl," Noah said insincerely, giving me another jab that he turned into a tickle. "Hey, Dad, can I use the car tonight?"

Daddy made a big production of digging through all his overall pockets, pulling his usual joke of trying to make Noah think we no longer owned car keys.

Meanwhile, Luke, my six-year-old brother, piped, "We're learning about presidents in school!" Luke looked owl-like, his eyes round and huge behind his glasses and the breeze ruffling his light-brown hair into feathers. "George Washington is the father of our country! He cut down a cherry tree but said, 'I cannot tell a lie'!"

First grade is a humongous deal to Luke. We always nod and smile and act impressed when he spouts out this kind of information.

"Keys, Dad?" Noah stuck his hand across the table, jiggling his fingers.

Daddy threw the keys to him, then leaned forward on his elbows and looked at me.

"Carly Barly, you're awful quiet tonight. What's new and exciting in *your* life?"

"I have to do an interview report about Dustin Groat," I answered, trying to pack the grimness of the situation into that one sentence.

"*The* Dustin Groat?" Noah hooted. "Remember when you used to come home from school, Carl, and try to get me to go beat Dustin Groat up? Or have him arrested?"

I rolled my eyes. That was ancient history, from three whole years ago. Third grade.

Daddy chuckled. "I remember. Here you were, Carly Barly, this little bitty thing, jumping around like a toad with pure anger. Seemed like Dustin Groat was all you talked about for a good while there."

I licked apricot off my thumb, not looking directly at either of them. "Well, Dustin kicked things all the time in Miss Tyleson's class," I said. "Sometimes even people. He head butted us on the slide ladder. *And* he kept pretending he chewed tobacco and spit on things. He kept spitting on the table and drawing with the spit, on the table where I sat, too. Once he spit right on Alicia's shoe on the playground. He was totally obnoxious."

"Remember what I used to tell you back then, to try and calm you down some?" Daddy asked.

Before I could answer him or even think about that, a low, scary thrumming blotted out the familiar sound of combines humming through the September fields on all sides of us. Luke popped up to his knees on the picnic bench, pointing over Mom's head.

"Helicopters!" he exclaimed.

Daddy shook his head. "More 'copters, all right. Going towards the river bottom."

"Ooooo, the *river bottom*, Carl!" Noah leaned toward my ear as three black shadows passed over our yard. "Swamp fiends that walk the night. The Jerome Monster, looking for his decapitated hand. Rabid dogs with poisonous fangs long as your thumb!"

I elbowed him like he had me, trying not to giggle. "Quit it!" I whispered. "I don't believe your dumb stories any longer, but you'll scare Luke. And for your information, you can't even decapitate a hand. Just a head."

"What?" Luke asked eagerly.

Noah just grinned his usual innocent grin, the one Mom says he inherited from Daddy and they both use to get away with murder. For the millionth time I wondered why Mom's blue eyes and Daddy's straight dark hair looked so great on him and so ordinary on me.

"I'm outta here," Noah announced, swinging his endless legs over the bench, then trotting backward toward the car. "Thanks, Dad!"

Mom called, "Noah, now you be . . ."

"I'll be careful and home by ten, Mom!"

"I wonder who the girl is tonight," Mom murmured to Daddy, shaking her head but smiling. She stood and started stacking the plates. Luke began his token job of collecting the napkins, crumpling them importantly against his chest like they were going to come to life and try to escape.

Daddy was still staring at the helicopters, which were tiny and toylike now as they disappeared over Koshkanong Woods. "Carly Barly, I remember the day you won that poetry contest in your class last year. You came running out to the machine shed to tell me about it that afternoon, all excited." He looked from the sky back down to me. "I'll never forget what you said that day. You told me your favorite thing about writing something was that it was like taking a trip, reaching a different exciting place each time."

I rolled my eyes. "Nice try, Daddy. But Dustin won't be an exciting trip."

He stood and stretched, then winked at me. "Well, C.B., I best get back out to the combining. Good luck on that report about your old nemesis."

Inside the house, before I had to start drying the dishes, I hurried to my room and quickly looked up nemesis. It meant "inevitable retribution," two strange words I only halfway knew and which would have taken twice as long to look up as nemesis itself had.

I was settling Luke into his bus seat up front by his friend Bryce the next morning when Randi leaned into the aisle and called, "Hurry, Carly! I've got an idea! Hustle so I can tell you about it!"

I came on down the aisle, flopped down beside her, and heeled my book bag under our seat. "An idea about our interview papers?"

"No, silly! An idea about jazz dancing!" She shook back her hair and bounced in our seat, all excited. "I can teach you and Alicia some dance moves, then the three of us can audition to do our act for Mr. Norville's Maple Leaf Days assembly next month!"

"Our . . . act?"

But Randi had clamped her Walkman over her ears and didn't hear me. Meanwhile, the bus stopped at the bottom of Alicia's long lane, and I turned my knees sideways for her to slip into her place between me and Randi.

"Do you think we'll work on our interviews as soon as class starts this morning?" I immediately asked her, partly to shove the idea of dancing out of my mind.

"Uh, probably," Alicia said, then swallowed and looked quickly down to smooth her tights. Something was up. When Alicia's feeling guilty, her freckles stand out, and that morning they seemed to be practically trying to escape from her face.

"You're lucky," I told her, "drawing a girl's name to interview. Cassie should be easy. She's got that glass unicorn collection and plays basketball and everything."

"Um, well, actually . . . I'm interviewing Randi now," Alicia said, rushing through the last four words: "And Randi's interviewing me."

I felt stunned, but I knew Alicia wasn't to blame. I leaned across Ali to snatch Randi's earphones off. "Since when are you two interviewing each other?" I demanded.

"Ow!" Randi whined, rubbing her ears. "Carly, it's no big deal. Okay, Krista had Cameron, and Cameron wanted Michael Jinson to have him, so Michael had Alicia and he traded her for Cameron. Then since Krista wanted Jasmine, she traded me Alicia. And Alicia had Cassie but Cassie wanted Todd and Todd had me, so Alicia traded Cassie to Todd and now I have Alicia and Alicia has me, that's all."

I was so hurt I could hardly talk, but I tried a little test to be sure I wasn't jumping to conclusions.

"But it was your idea, right, Randi? You figured out how everybody could get their best friend—Michael Jinson and Cameron, Krista and Jasmine, and you and Alicia."

"Right, and Todd and Cassie like each other, so that worked out just perfectly, too."

"Thank you very much for the information," I said. Was it possible she hadn't heard herself agreeing that she and Ali were best friends, when the three of us had been equal best friends since before kindergarten? It was almost like she was *trying* to keep things unequal!

I turned my back to them so my feet were in the aisle and I flipped open my writing notebook.

"Carly, are you mad? You can't get mad at us just because you got stuck with creepy Dustin, who nobody would even think of trading for!"

"Would you please keep your voice down, Randi?" I requested. "Some of us have to prepare for real interviews, not merely write down a ton of stuff we've already known about the other one for a million years."

I heard them whispering, and then Alicia tapped my shoulder and said timidly, "Uh, Carl, we better tell you one more thing. You know how Cassie had you? Well, Dustin had Todd but Todd wanted Cassie to have him, so Todd told Dustin that instead he has to have you now."

"Fine!" I scrunched shut my eyes. "Just fine, fine, fine!"

But it wasn't fine—not one bit. I positively hated the

idea of being interviewed by Dustin Groat. One of two things would happen. Either he would just sit there, looking at his desk and not asking anything at all, or he would ask a bunch of sarcastic, gross, and humiliating stuff.

And either thing would be horrible.

three

When Ms. Aspen told us to move for interview time that morning, I forced myself to walk back to Dustin's corner, dragging a desk from the last row behind me. Like the day before, Dustin was slouched in his usual state of suspended animation, his heavy boots far out in front of him in a puddle of dirt, his arms folded like Ms. Aspen hadn't given a word of instruction. He didn't even move his feet when the bottom of my desk nearly smashed right into his legs.

I sat down, cleared my throat, and opened my notebook. "Do you want to interview me first, or should I interview you first?" I asked him.

My heart was beating so hard it hurt.

Dustin folded his arms on his desk and put his forehead down on them. The small gold safety pin in his knuckle glinted in the sun.

"Okay, I'll go first then," I said politely. I kept telling myself to relax, that things would be all right, but I didn't really believe this because things were starting off far worse than I'd expected. I took a deep breath. "Question number one. What is your name?"

"Superman," Dustin grumbled to his desk.

Dustin Groat, I wrote after my first question.

"When were you born?"

For a long time, he didn't answer. He finally mumbled, "It was cold. It must have been the winter."

That took me by surprise. I was expecting a dumb Superman date, like *the year 3067, Krypton time.* But was he being sarcastic?

"Well, I meant, when's your birthday . . . uh, birthdate?"

"November thirtieth," Dustin said to his desk. He hunched up his left shoulder and scrunched his ear down onto it.

November 30, I wrote. "So, you're eleven?"

"I'll be thirteen in two months," he said, bouncing his forehead on his folded arms, up and down, up and down. Suddenly, he winced and sat up, clamping his left hand over his left ear.

"What's wrong?" I whispered.

He yanked a grungy pencil from inside his desk and broke the lead point off with his thumbnail. Normally the idea of actually touching Dustin would have made me gag, but I automatically reached out and grabbed his wrist just as he started to stick that splintery thing into his ear again like he had the day before.

"Don't!" I whispered. "I mean it! Just . . . don't!"

He froze with the pencil an inch from his ear, like I'd turned him to stone. Only his eyes moved, flickered up from his desk to me, then down again.

I felt everybody around us moving, so I jerked my hand back to my lap. But no one was looking at us, thank goodness. Everybody had just turned to stare out the row of windows above the science table. Four black helicopters had appeared over the playground like humongous wasps.

"I've seen more helicopters this past week than I've seen before in my entire life," I told Dustin, needing something—anything!—to say. "My dad says they're going to the river bottom."

Dustin turned to glare out the window. "They should mind their own business," he snarled.

Their own business? What was *that* supposed to mean? And why was he so mad? On top of how nervous I already was, I suddenly had this horrible feeling he might be about to spit on the floor, like clear back in third grade.

"It's no big deal," I said, thinking, *Please, please don't spit!* "They're probably just practicing where nobody can get hurt if they crash. Nobody below them, I mean, since nothing's out along the river bottom but the gross, smelly landfill and snakey old Jerome Swamp."

Dustin's face was white as he kept his eyes like lasers

on those helicopters. He had his hand cupped over his ear and was pressing it with tiny little pulses. Otherwise, nothing about him was moving. Nothing.

His stillness was weird, dark and scary. It made you realize how much all the other boys in our class constantly moved—jiggled their feet, their elbows, their knees.

Think of something! I ordered my brain. *Make that silence go away! Say anything!*

"When my friends and I were younger, my brother told us these really dumb stories about the river bottom," I babbled. "For instance, he made up stories about this horrible pack of demon dogs that ran along the edge of the river, biting people and turning them into . . ."

Dustin leaned toward me across his desk, fast as a striking snake. His eyes were cold and hard as a snake's eyes, too, and I caught my breath and flinched.

"Raving lunatics. That's what they turned into," he said in a hoarse whisper. "In the back room there's screws in the floorboards, clear through four inches of oak. Six screws, three on each side. That's where the bed stood in the old days. That's where our people was put as they died of the swamp rabies. They strapped them down with leather straps that were screwed to the floor. Had to, or they'd have torn their own faces off. They was raving lunatics by the time they died. Raving insane with foam coming from their mouths."

I swallowed. Really, it was more of a big, loud gulp.

19

"There's more than 'nothing' at the river bottom," Dustin said, then slithered quietly back to slouch in his chair. "There's always been *us* out there, too."

So the Groats actually *lived* out where Flat River became Jerome Swamp? They actually lived where nobody else's parents would even let their kids ride bikes, because of the burning landfill and the huge mosquitoes and snakes and slime and who knew what other awful things hiding in the polluted mist and mud?

I watched that silence wrap around Dustin again like a thick, dark coat.

Then I bent my head and pretended to write, though I could barely breathe, let alone think. Interview time was surely almost over. Surely.

The intercom speaker above the front blackboard suddenly crackled to life. "Attention, Ms. Aspen, Nurse Jasper needs two of your students, Tyler Christenson and Dustin Groat, to come to the health room immediately, please."

"Tyler! Dustin!" Ms. Aspen clapped her hands with the eager, hurry-up look on her face that teachers always have when the intercom gives them an order, and slowly Dustin got up and stalked down the aisle.

I stared for a minute at Dustin's empty chair, thinking, *Get a grip, Carly, this is only Dustin, not some creature from the swamp!*

I shuddered one hard shudder, then walked back to my own seat.

★   ★   ★

"Dustin Groat has a bug living in his left ear," Randi eagerly stated to everyone at our table at lunch that day. "That's why Nurse Jasper called him out of class."

Everybody got wide-eyed, and Krista looked green.

"It's totally, totally gross!" Randi went on.

I rolled my eyes and dropped my spoon.

Jasmine gurgled her last slurp of milk up through her straw, then asked, "How'd you find out about it, Randi?"

Randi shrugged. "When I went into the office to look in the lost and found for my geography book just now, everybody was talking about it. Three teachers who were in there, Nurse Jasper, even the custodians. Nurse Jasper had to use special *instruments* to get it out. That's how deep in his head it was. Or is. I'm not sure whether she got it or whether it, like, squirmed away from her instruments, deeper into his brain."

Jasmine choked on her milk. I tore off a small corner of my burrito, but it looked so much like an ear that I grimaced and dropped it into my applesauce.

Stuff Randi says tends to get around fast. By that afternoon, practically everybody seemed to know about the earbug. Dustin didn't even bother denying it, though he kept telling people over and over again that it was gone.

"Nurse Jasper drug it out with a pair of tweezers, then pinched it to death and threw it away in a piece of Kleenex!" he angrily insisted when people kept run-

21

ning up during afternoon recess, looking into his ear. "Go ask her yourself if you don't believe me, stupidos! Go see for yourself in her trash can!"

But no matter what Dustin said or how much he slapped and batted and even kicked them away, most people didn't really believe the bug was gone and kept on sneaking up, hoping.

Right after school, this cute boy in our class named Joey Snyder cornered Dustin between the side of the school and the bike racks. "At least tell us how big it is," Joey ordered. "I mean, is it as big as a medium-size bug, like a cockroach, or small, like a mosquito? Here." Joey smoothed out the playground dirt with his tennis shoe. "Draw it." He picked up a stick and thrust it into Dustin's face.

All of us gathered around.

Dustin's yellowish-orange hair was sweat-spiked, and his neck was splotchy red. Joey was taller, and his shiny dark hair fell neatly from a part that was as white and even as a chalk line.

Joey seemed almost like a grown-up right then, like you had to do what he said.

Dustin seemed like a trapped animal with glittering eyes.

Finally, Dustin grabbed the stick, but instead of drawing with it he stuck it in his mouth like a bone. Then he bit it in half and spit it out. Then he spit on the ground. Then he yelled, "Stupido! You want some more where that came from? I'll give you something to

22

scream about if that's all you can do, stupido! Just scream your heads off and see if anybody hears or cares!"

He kicked the gravel into a dusty swirl and spit again.

"He's acting so *different,*" Alicia whispered to me. "All that yelling and kicking. He's usually so . . . you know, quiet. And broody."

"He's acting like a nemesis again, like clear back in third grade!" I whispered back.

"A what?" Jasmine asked.

"Somebody obnoxious that tries to drive you crazy," I told her, going with my instincts since the dictionary definition had made no sense.

"Of course, people usually leave him alone in his corner and don't poke at him with sticks," Alicia added quietly.

We all kept watching in disbelief as Dustin Groat turned and sped around the corner of the school, to the parking lot side that belonged to the high schoolers.

Everyone gasped. No one had dared to go over there before.

four

What did you creepy sixth graders do to Dustin Groat today?" Noah asked when we were doing our chores in the barnyard that night.

I shrugged and went on filling the chickens' water containers with the hose. Noah took out his pocket knife so he could cut the twine from a hay bale he was getting ready to put out for the cows.

"We just wanted him to draw this bug Nurse Jasper found in his ear," I finally answered.

Noah shook his head. "Yeah, I heard about you guys and that stupid nonexistent bug."

"It's not nonexistent," I told him. I looped the hose over the edge of the horse trough and stood up to stretch. "And what did *you* guys do to Dustin?"

"What are you talking about?" he asked.

Like I'd expected, he wasn't about to admit to the

torture you faced if you dared to enter senior-high territory.

"Noah, if a bug got in your ear, could it walk right through the inside of your skull and come out the other ear?"

Noah laughed. "No way! Hey, people's heads are crammed full of their brains and stuff. There'd be no room for even a bug to squeeze through." He grabbed the bale and grunted it to his chest, then shoved it over the fence.

"That's what I thought." I swallowed. "But, well, if it had sharp pinchers, couldn't it, like . . . gnaw its way through?" I asked him that because I kept wondering why Dustin Groat had told Joey and those guys that he'd make them scream. Scream wasn't a word the other boys used. The ones who wanted to seem gross and tough said things like, "I'll beat you to a pulp!" or "I'll kick your face in!" The word scream didn't seem threatening enough. Unless it meant something worse when Dustin said it, like he'd heard himself scream while his brain was being gnawed.

Noah swung himself over the fence and started kicking the bale ahead of him, toward the feeder. "You read too many scary books, Carly. They're warping your mind!"

I rushed over and climbed the fence, too, then hung with my arms braced over the top rung. "I asked you about that because I'm doing the most important report of my whole life, and I'm doing it on Dustin! He's such a horrible person that it didn't even enter my head I might get him, but I did. So since there's nothing interesting in a neat way about him, I have to think of something interesting in a gross way. Like, for instance, him being brain-tortured by an out-of-control earbug."

Noah started walking back, wiping the hay dust from his hands onto his jeans. "What's so important about this report, anyhow?" he asked.

I took a deep breath, let it out, and bounced my chin on the fence rail. "Noah, if you saw Ali and Randi and me together, would you think we were supposed to be? Together, I mean?"

He snorted a laugh. "I can't imagine you guys not together."

I licked my lips. "Alicia's so tiny and cute, and she's the best gymnast on the gymnastics team. And Randi's, well, got this new satellite dish and stuff. People say Joey Snyder, you know . . . likes her."

Noah just stood there leaning on the fence next to me, frowning. "So what's that got to do with this Dustin report having to be gross?"

"It has to be good, Noah! Not gross—good, though to be good it will have to be gross since it can't be . . . good. Oh, Noah, don't you get it? Ali's a gymnast, Randi's a dancer, and I'm a . . . what? I have to be editor, Noah! I just have to be!"

Like I figured he would, Noah just shook his head and laughed a little, then walked over to get another bale.

26

"Noah," I called, "you say I warp my mind with scary books, but *you* made up those swamp-fiend stories! And those demon dogs!" I swallowed. "I mean . . . uh, you *did* just make that stuff up, right, Noah?"

"*I* didn't make up those stories, Carl," he called back. "People around here have been telling stories like that about the river bottom forever."

He was bending over the bale, ready to pick it up.

"Well, the Groats actually *live* somewhere along the river bottom," I told him. "Bet you didn't know that. In your dumb stories you said *nobody* could live out where those swamp fiends wander around and . . . Noah?"

He'd let go of the bale and was leaning forward, his hands braced on the rough hay for balance. He turned, flopped down to sit on the bale, and put his elbows on his knees.

My usually laid-back brother was suddenly acting like I'd kicked him in the stomach instead of giving him a simple piece of information. "Noah?"

"Yeah, yeah, Carl, I know perfectly well where the Groats live. Just finish your chores, okay?" he mumbled, putting his head in his hands.

When I got back to the house, Mom was sitting on the porch swing, peeling apples. Luke was on his stomach on the floor near her, propped up on his elbows with our cat, Twinkletoes, sleeping on the backs of his legs. As I trudged up the four porch stairs, I saw that he had his first-grade tablet open on the floor and he was painstakingly making capital *E*'s and *F*'s and *G*'s between the turquoise and pink lines.

"What's with Noah?" I asked Mom. "He's acting strange."

"Noah?" Mom shrugged. "Probably just hungry."

"Carly, walk softer! You're jiggling my pencil!" Luke scolded me.

I sighed and sat down on the top step. "Sorry. But you're wasting your time learning perfect penmanship anyway," I told him. "You'd be better off learning how to be funny or good at some sport or something. Being good at flashy things and cuteness are what really count in life."

Mom quickly looked over at me. A second later she held out a piece of apple between her thumb and the knife, and I got up to take it and to sit beside her on the swing.

"Randi just called," she said. "She wanted to remind you to wear shorts tomorrow so she can start teaching you to . . . jazz dance."

Again, I sighed. "She wants us to be in Mr. Norville's program next month." I wedged my heels between the two wide-spaced floorboards and rocked us back and forth, nibbling my apple section.

"Looking forward to that?" she asked. "Dancing, I mean?"

I shrugged. "Randi is, and Alicia sort of wants to learn, and we always do stuff together. The three of us."

She didn't say anything back, and I figured I'd go on

upstairs to my room. But instead I sat pushing us back and forth, listening to the rhythmic squeak of the moving swing.

After a minute, she handed me another apple slice.

"I always felt it was so lucky you and Randi and Alicia lived so close together," she said softly, "but I always wondered a little, different as you were, if you'd still be close friends when you got older. You have to be yourself, Carly. Sometimes you have to put what really matters to you ahead of some other things."

I turned to her. "Mom, do you know any real poets? I mean, do you know how poets look? Randi's been wearing these little flouncy skirts like a real dancer this year. And Ali sometimes wears leotards and gym shorts and this charm necklace shaped like a girl doing a handstand. I think if I can *look* more like a writer, maybe . . ." I shrugged, not sure how to finish the sentence.

Mom looked at me without saying anything. Then, after a minute, she took my right hand and rubbed the writing bump on the knuckle of my middle finger with her thumb.

"Writers have these," she said softly, and smiled.

But that wasn't what I meant, of course.

five

As I planned my interview questions that night, I decided to try to get Dustin to tell me a lot more gross things about where he lived. Of course, that approach to making my report what Ms. Aspen had called "in-depth" was risky. I mean, every sixth-grade boy would have given me the editor job in a second for describing those raving, strapped-down lunatics in vivid detail, but teachers were a different matter.

It took me more than an hour to think of questions that wouldn't be insulting. Even something like, "What's it like, living in a swamp?" might sound rude. "Is it hard to breathe with the smell of burning garbage from the landfill around you all the time?" might be even worse.

★   ★   ★

By the time Ms. Aspen told us to move into inter-view position the next morning, I had three very care-fully worded questions written out. That kind of advance preparation usually makes me less nervous about things, but as I pulled my desk against Dustin's and rummaged through to the right section of my note-book, I noticed my hands were shaking.

I glanced at Dustin, who was looking at his desk. I cleared my throat and looked back down at my first question. "Okay, question number one. What's your ad-dress?"

Dustin stayed slumped. Even his eyes didn't move.

"Why don't you ask them black 'copters where we live at," he finally mumbled, still without moving or looking up.

That made no sense, so I didn't write it down.

"Well, like, I mean, if the UPS man has a package to deliver, what address would you give him over the phone?" I asked in a calm voice. Meanwhile, I was push-ing my pencil point into the paper of my notebook so hard it was making a hole.

"There's no phone," Dustin muttered, and put his head down on his desk. He bounced his forehead up and down, up and down.

No phone, I wrote.

"Okay, next question. Were you born at this, uh . . . compound?"

I felt a nervous flutter in my stomach. I was taking a chance, calling where he lived a compound. Was that a

31

bad word? I should have looked it up, since I only sort of knew what one was. Everyone, including the newspaper, said "the Groat compound," but could you call it that to their faces?

He shrugged his shoulders, still bouncing his head.

"So you don't know where you were born?" I asked.

He shook his head, bouncing it side to side.

Unknown, I wrote, irritated. Everybody knows where they were born.

Dustin shoved up the floppy sleeve of his shirt and began scratching a cluster of mosquito bites right over his left elbow. I caught my breath—there *was* a tattoo up there, halfway between his elbow and his shoulder! There was a red rectangle with an *X* of star-studded blue across it. I quickly sketched that design into my notes.

"In the back of a truck," Dustin said.

"What?"

"I was born in the back of a truck."

Swallowing, I put a comma after *Unknown* and added *but in the back of a truck.*

"Who . . . who is your mother?" I asked.

Dustin sat up, crossed his right leg over his left leg, and began slowly twisting the safety pin that was stuck through his knuckle. He closed his eyes, grimacing.

"She been gone a long time," he said, his voice so gravelly I thought at first he'd given me some long, weird name, like Sheba Gonnalong Thyme.

Then, with his eyes still clamped shut, he started kicking the leg of my desk, hard. Each kick was far apart and separate, the kind of kicks you couldn't keep from counting in your head. They jolted me, and I dug my heels into the floor to keep my desk from inching backward.

One . . . two . . . three . . . four . . . five . . . six . . . seven . . . eight . . . nine.

By the time he stopped, so much dirt had shaken off his boot that the floor beneath me looked even grungier than the floor beneath his own desk.

"Dustin Groat!" Ms. Aspen made Dustin's name sound like a massive sneeze when she yelled it out like that.

I about jumped out of my skin. I'd been in another world, and that sound brought me crashing back to class.

Ms. Aspen sent Dustin to Ms. Trinny's office for kicking school property. A couple of minutes later, Randi got permission to go to the office, too—to ask if she and Ali and I could go to the gym during noon recess to start practicing jazz dancing.

"What did Ms. Trinny do to Dustin?" I asked Randi in the rest room right before lunch.

Randi shrugged. "I didn't see him. I waited in the outside office for about fifteen minutes while Ms. Trinny yelled at him, though."

"Yelled at him? Yell-yelled, or just talk-yelled?"

"Randi, are we practicing in the gym or not?" Alicia interrupted.

"We are," Randi said. "Except, listen, don't either of you mention to anyone that we haven't auditioned for Mr. Norville's program yet, okay?"

"You *guys*!" I demanded, exasperated.

They both looked at me, and I felt a little flustered. I wanted to bring the subject back to Dustin, but I couldn't do that without them wondering why I was making such a big deal of it. Why was I, anyway?

"Why can't we say we haven't auditioned for Mr. Norville yet?" I finished, weakly.

"Because I may have sort of told Ms. Trinny that Mr. Norville wants us to practice in the gym."

"You lied to the principal," I pointed out, flabbergasted.

But she just shrugged. "Not really. Of course Mr. Norville will want us to perform once he sees our act, and once we're performing he'll be thrilled that we've been practicing each day, so I just rearranged the order of things."

I'd expected to feel self-conscious and miserable dancing in the gym after lunch, but we had it all to ourselves, so I could relax and not worry. The big overhead lights were off, and the small windows that ran all along the top of the walls were filled with softly moving sunlight from the tossing trees outside.

34

Before I knew it, I was pretty much ignoring the bossy instructions Randi was giving. I'd kicked off my shoes and was simply gliding and spinning through the flickering shadows in time to the music on Randi's tape player.

Then suddenly the junior high basketball boys came charging in to practice. And though they stayed clear over on the other half of the gym, shooting toward the hoop that was near the stage, everything, just everything, immediately changed.

For one thing, Alicia became robotic. I mean, her dance movements had been perfect from the second Randi showed her—almost too perfect. More like gymnastics moves than what you'd call true dance. But when the basketball boys came in she got so perfect she seemed like this boring little mechanical ballerina in my music box at home.

And Randi! When the basketball boys came in, Randi became unbelievable.

She was always telling us that she was a natural dancer because she had "attitude." Well, when the basketball boys came in, she went from having attitude to just sort of slopping tons of attitude all over the place.

"Five, six, seven, *eight!*" she started barking out, loud enough to be heard five miles away, snapping her fingers and tossing her hair so I don't know how she could see an inch in front of her. And *then* she started crashing down every so often into what she must have

35

thought were splits, though she wasn't going down nearly far enough for them to be real splits.

"The audience can see your underwear," I finally pointed out. She had shorts on, but still, it was the principal of the thing. "And every time you get back up from that position you look really stupid."

I was only trying to keep her from making a fool of herself, but about the third time I told her that, Randi marched over and turned off the tape player, then faced me with her hands on her hips.

"Carly, what *is* your problem? All you've done for the past ten minutes is stand there rolling your eyes at me and Alicia!"

I kept swallowing hard, over and over, but still my forehead burned. "I can't stand dancing in front of the basketball boys, Randi! I mean, just . . . just because you and Alicia are so good at stuff this year, you think . . . you think you can rig the interviews and everything and it just makes me want to scream because it's my editor audition you're ruining, Randi, *mine*, did that ever even occur to you? I mean, you said yourself I should be editor, but do you even care that it's my big chance you're ruining?"

She shook her head, looking confused. "What's the interview assignment got to do with you calling me stupid in front of the team?"

The bell began ringing, and Randi grabbed up her shoes and Alicia's. She stomped over and grabbed Alicia by the elbow.

"Come on, Ali, we'll practice *our* act again tomorrow afternoon at my house, when some people who think they're too smart for us aren't standing around in the way, giving us criticism!"

Half-tiptoeing, half-running, Alicia let Randi pull her along toward the gym doors. She looked back at me over her shoulder, but I couldn't see her freckles well enough to tell if she was mad or just upset.

The basketball boys thundered out, too, leaving the gym unbelievably quiet. I crept over and sat near my tennis shoes with my back pressed against the cold tile of the wall that separated the gym from the hallway. I picked up one shoe and looked into the cavelike entrance under the tongue, wishing I could just crawl inside and stay there.

Then suddenly something moved in my peripheral vision. I turned sharply in that direction just in time to see Dustin Groat slink out from underneath the long row of bleachers to stand in the dark triangle of shadow at the bleachers' edge.

He'd been in the gym the whole time we had, spying on us!

six

No one was allowed in the gym without permission, but Dustin had sneaked in anyway and hidden under the bleachers. He'd even been watching me sitting there all alone for the past two minutes, staring miserably into my shoe! It made me feel nauseous for a few seconds, but then I realized the bleachers were so far away and the gym was so murky he probably didn't even notice that anyone was still here.

Then something totally bizarre happened that made me positive he didn't know anyone was still in the gym.

Still standing in that triangle of deep shadow, Dustin Groat suddenly began talking to himself.

"Don't be scared, don't be scared. I won't let them snatch at you nor harm you. Nobody will lay a hand to you while I've got breath in my body to stop them."

I could hear him perfectly, though he spoke in a quiet

mumble. The empty gym grabbed every sound and amplified it.

"You're safe. Ain't nobody gonna come after you 'cause ain't nobody knows where you be. Just hug close, now, and we'll make a run for it on out of here before they see us. You ready?"

Then Dustin began a bulletlike dash out of the deep shadows and toward the big double doors that led into the hallway. Those double doors were only a few yards from where I sat, and halfway to them he saw me and stopped in his tracks like a forest creature caught in somebody's headlights.

Because I'd turned to watch his escape, my left ear was right against the wall now, and the tiles must have magnified the sounds on the other side. Suddenly I was bombarded by the voices of the boys in our class, who hang around out in the hall after the first bell, waiting till the last possible second to hustle into our classroom.

"So, like, my mother said if I keep pulling on my toes while I watch TV and stuff, my toe joints will get, like, really big? Like your finger joints get really big if you keep cracking your knuckles? So I'm not supposed to do it any more?"

That was Adam Gerber.

"Yeah, but, so what? I mean, so, like, she has to buy you bigger tennis shoes, big deal," Joey Snyder said back. "She's probably just cheap."

I jumped to my feet, waving my arms and shaking my head wildly.

"Go back!" I whisper-shouted to Dustin. "Don't open those doors! Joey's right outside! Wait till he goes on into class!"

Dustin looked from me to the double doors, then ran backward the way he'd come, like a hermit crab scurrying inside its shell. When he was all the way under the bleachers again, I slipped my feet into my shoes and quickly left the gym, my heart pounding a mile a minute.

What had I been *thinking?* You didn't warn people like Dustin Groat, especially when they'd just been spying on you and your friends!

As I sat in class that afternoon, concentrating on not paying any attention to Alicia (to my left) or Randi (right behind me), I decided to abandon forever the silly and juvenile world of dance and to dedicate myself completely to my own higher art form—poetry. In fact, I labeled the front of my shoulder notebook *Poetry Book*. I wrote that title in balloon letters with my green marker, and filled each of the letters in with tiny purple stars.

On the bus going home I had to sit in my normal seat, since there were no empty seats. But I kept my face turned toward the aisle and my back completely to Randi and Ali.

"Her heart just wasn't in the act," I heard Randi gossiping behind me.

"Would you please keep your voices down?" I requested without turning around. "I happen to be writing, and poetry isn't something you can do without even halfway thinking about it, like jazz dancing."

But Randi wouldn't even honor a polite request.

"Her bad attitude is what got her cut from the squad," she practically yelled to Alicia. "She'd have to promise not to be so critical if she wanted back on."

"The squad?!" I just had to laugh scornfully over my shoulder. "You call that little two-person act a *squad?*"

I don't know what else they said because I bent down, put my elbows on my knees, clamped my hands over my ears, and started humming the National Anthem.

I meant to spend all weekend setting up an official poetry studio in the hayloft and working on my writerly wardrobe, one that was sophisticated enough to prove to everyone how really juvenile jazz dancing was. But on Saturday morning I realized that the only thing I knew about writer clothes was that writers wore mainly black, so I needed black dye.

I saw Noah walking toward the machinery shed to putter on this hopeless old car he'd bought from one of his friends for fifty dollars and was trying to get running. I rushed out to the porch and yelled, "Noah, will you take me to Wal-Mart real quick so I can get some school stuff? I'll do your dishes tonight."

He shrugged and nodded. Noah is pathetically easy to bribe on his dish days.

We took Daddy's truck, since Mom needed the car.

You don't waste your breath and energy trying to talk above the loud, hiccuping motor when the truck is moving, but when we got to the little bridge over Koshkanong Creek, Noah pulled to the side of the road and leaned out his window, trying to see something back in the woods.

"What?" I asked, looking over his shoulder. There were deep and muddy truck tracks leading from the road to the edge of the woods, and a small pile of beer cans glittered like silver nuggets at each end of those tracks.

Noah shook his head. "The Groats were out here partying last night. I heard them when I came home from my soccer game. They had a big old fire going, too, right out in the middle of the woods." He sighed. "Could have started a real forest fire. And why do they have to leave such a mess everywhere they go?"

I licked my lips. "Uh, Noah? Speaking of the Groats, you know that important report I'm doing about Dustin? Well, I've never seen where he lives, in fact I'm not so sure exactly what a compound even is, so I was wondering, while we're already out and everything, if after we go to Wal-Mart, we could . . ."

Noah jerked around to face me. "Don't even ask, Carl. Dad would have a fit if I took you out to the river bottom. It's just too weird. Some of my friends have snuck out there this fall, and they say the Groats *do* have a drug lab. Jake says you can smell it and see this strange green smoke coming out of . . ."

"Please, Noah? Oh, Noah, please, please, please?"

He just shook his head. "No. N-O, no, Carl."

"I don't even think they have a drug lab." I crossed my arms and stared stubbornly out the window. "I'd have to actually see that green smoke to believe it."

But Noah didn't take the bait. "Nice try, Carl, but it's no use going out there."

"No use? What's that supposed to mean?"

Noah gulped and suddenly got as pale as he had the afternoon when I'd first mentioned the Groats' living at the river bottom. Long red streaks appeared on each side of his neck. Something was *definitely* going on with him, and it wasn't, like Mom had guessed, just hunger.

I bounced in my seat. "Oh, Noah, come on! Please? I'll do your dishes all three times next week."

Noah closed his eyes and put his head back against the seat.

"You know what, Noah? I think you're scared. You kid me about reading scary books, but I think you're the one who believes those dumb stories about the swamp."

"Yeah, right, Carl," he murmured without opening his eyes.

His mysterious stubbornness was starting to make me mad. I'd tried begging him, not believing him, bribing him, and even ridiculing him. What was left?

Then Noah slowly sat up straight, rubbed his eyes, and turned to look directly at me. I was shocked. Unless I was seeing things wrong, there was a strange, eager look on his face now. Actually, he looked eager and scared at once, like spies look in movies while they sneak into the enemy stronghold.

"Dad'll get suspicious if we're gone too long," he said.

"Then let's just skip Wal-Mart and do this!" I urged, grabbing his arm.

He took a deep breath and let it out. "I tried not to," I barely heard him whisper to himself as he put the truck in gear. "Nobody can say I didn't try."

seven

We drove into Cooper's Glade, then past the school and the grocery store and the post office. Noah turned left, then right again, and we drove past some houses in a part of town I couldn't remember ever being in before. Finally we were out in the country, but not country like where *we* live.

The land was suddenly very flat, and there weren't many trees. There was trash in the muddy ditches. I was a little surprised that things could get ugly so fast, with nothing working up to it or anything.

"There's the county landfill," Noah yelled over the noise of the motor, nodding toward a huge pit to our right, off the road a little way, and filled with burning junk.

Past the landfill, Noah turned left, then right again, and we were suddenly driving parallel to Flat River.

The few raggedy trees along the bank trailed off into a bunch of muddy stumps, and a high, rusty fence began along the side of the road a few feet from where we drove. Flat River was suddenly as hidden from view as if it didn't exist.

"Behind that fence is the Groat property," Noah yelled, downshifting and grinding the gears.

I leaned forward to see across him. The fence bulged and sagged. Things had been propped up against it, mostly old car doors and stacks of muddy tires. In one place, an old refrigerator had been turned on its side to plug a huge hole gaping where the fence should have met the ground. Six black-and-white spotted pigs and a few frowsy chickens had sneaked under the fence and were rooting and pecking around in the muddy ditch between it and the road.

Signs had been hung all along the fence, big pieces of gray board spray-painted with bright, misspelled words: KEEP AWAY! THIS MEENS YOU and MIND YOR OWN BIZNESS and even one that read WE SHOOT FIRST AND AX QUESTIONS LATER.

We passed another sign, this one truly shocking. RABBID DOGS! KEEP OUT!

"Noah, they've got dogs with rabies in there!"

He glanced at the sign and shook his head, chuckling uneasily. "Don't worry, Carl—there hasn't been a case of rabies out at the swamp in fifty years. That sign is just supposed to scare people away."

The fence wasn't wire any longer. Now it was made of

wood, mostly old road signs stuck up on their ends and more of those gray boards. It was too tall to see over.

"Then . . . what's back there?" I asked, still not totally convinced it wasn't awful drooling dogs that would leave you drooling and raving yourself, strapped into a hideous bed in the Groats' back room.

"Barns and sheds and junk. And wood piles. That's the Groats' line of work, selling wood." He glanced at me and added, with a snicker, "Their *legitimate* line of work."

The high board fence finally turned wire again, and ahead of us was a wide gate, padlocked shut across the muddy drive into the compound. Noah idled the truck so we were even with that gate and could get a look at what was beyond it. His hand was still on the gearshift knob. I could tell he was ready to peel out at a second's notice.

I slid around farther sideways in my seat, holding my breath. This was like watching a movie of a land so far away and strange that it took all your concentration and imagination to keep your bearings.

There was a long, squat house set far back in a muddy yard on the other side of the locked gate. Several shiny black motorcycles were gathered in front. The house was painted a dull green, and it reminded me of something, but I couldn't think of what. Some of the windows were broken. What looked like a pair of gray socks was stuffed into a round hole in one of them. The big picture window, where I figured the living room probably was, had a huge flag stretched across it instead of curtains—a red background with a star-spangled X of blue across it.

"Dustin's tattoo!" I exclaimed. I looked at Noah, and he looked at me. "Dustin has a tattoo that matches that flag!"

"That's the Confederate flag," Noah said quietly. "The Rebel flag from the Civil War."

Yes! I *knew* I'd seen it somewhere. Now I remembered pictures of it from our American history book.

"Why do they like the Confederate flag so much?" I asked Noah. For some reason, I was whispering.

"Dunno. Some of the Groats rode with Quantrill's Raiders during the Civil War. But that's ancient history."

"Who were Quantrill's Raiders?"

Noah didn't answer me, probably didn't hear me. There was just so much to take in. The wide, muddy yard was cluttered with wrecked cars and parts of cars, and with old washing machines and mattresses and things. Big black trash sacks were strung around, too. Lots of them were ripped open, and three skinny dogs were eating out of one. There was an old rusty plow with curved metal things like bony fingers scratching down into the mud, and near it was something small and fur-covered, squashed and lifeless.

"Is that . . ." A bitter taste was creeping up my throat, choking me. I hoped Noah would know what I was thinking and would say that was just a piece of loose fur and not a kitten.

But he didn't say anything.

The wind had come up and was banging things against the fence in an impatient, irritable way. There were other sounds, too—a motor being revved in one of the many old tin sheds, the squawk of chickens, loud country music on a radio. I heard people yelling to each other, or at each other. Then I heard a door bang, loud and metallic like a gunshot.

And suddenly Dustin Groat ran from around the back of the house, hunched and grimacing, holding his left ear against his shoulder. His left arm dangled in a stiff sort of way, too, and he was clutching it above the elbow with his right hand.

Breathe! I had to order myself before I remembered and gulped a deep lungful of thick, fish-smelling air.

Then a girl's sad face appeared in the corner of the window. She was looking out at Dustin, peeking from the edge of that red Rebel flag.

Dustin's house looked like a frog—that was it! The big, slick, and slimy kind. That Rebel flag looked like its fat open mouth, and it seemed to be trying to devour the girl in the window alive.

Dustin ran around in the space between his house and one of the sheds, kicking at the hard tufts of mud. He kicked one loose, tried to pick it up with his left hand, but dropped it. With his right hand he picked it up and threw it at his own house. The three dogs looked over at him for a second, then went back to sniffing things like this was nothing new.

A tall, skinny man came out of the house, holding a piece of wood in one hand. He stalked toward Dustin, but Dustin took one look at him and ran into one of the sheds.

As the dogs moved toward the kitten in the mud, I ordered myself to grab another shot of air, then I pounded Noah's shoulder. "Noah, let's go!"

But he was looking at the girl in the window and he seemed almost hypnotized. "Julie," he whispered. I glanced quickly back at the awful house, and the girl was staring at Noah, too.

"No-ah, we've got to *go! Now!*"

"Right," Noah said, shoving the truck into gear and finally hitting the gas.

eight

We tore down the road, the wide, bouncy truck tires gyrating wildly in the muddy, loose gravel. Noah took several quick turns to put us out of sight of the compound, cornering so wildly I braced my palms and then my knees against the dashboard. He didn't slow down till we were at least a couple of miles away from the river. Then he just hit the brake, slid the truck to a fishtailing stop, and put his forehead down on the steering wheel.

As road dust and the smell of burning tire rubber rose around us, I saw out the corner of my eye that his jaw muscles were clenching and unclenching and he was gripping the wheel so hard his sharp, bony knuckles looked white.

"Noah, uh . . . who was that girl?" I finally dared to ask. "That . . . Julie?"

He slowly sat up straight and rubbed his face hard with his hands, then stared sadly out the window.

"She was in my class," he said quietly, "until a couple of years ago, when they suddenly took her out of school. They said they needed her at home, to help raise Dustin. Julie's Dustin's sister."

"Dustin told me their mother's been gone a long time," I prodded.

Noah turned to me. "Three years. And not exactly gone. Dead. She drowned in Flat River the fall when Julie and I were in eighth grade. So why'd they wait till the next year to take Julie out of school, if needing her for Dustin was the real reason? Why didn't they do it when her mother first died, instead of right when we started going together in ninth grade?"

Thunk! His head hit the steering wheel again. "When I first got my license I used to keep driving by there, but I never saw her, not once," he mumbled in this whispery, pathetic way. "So I stay away from there now and keep trying to pretend she doesn't exist, just like everybody wants me to."

I'd never seen Noah acting like this. Not even when our dad caught him and his friends trying cigarettes in our barn and grounded him for an entire month. I couldn't think of a single thing to say, or do, to make him feel better, and finally, still looking dazed, he started the truck and drove us home.

*   *   *

Up in my room that afternoon, I sprawled on my stomach across my bed, thinking of what Noah had said when he'd had his lovesick fit in the truck. Dustin and Julie's mother had died, not just disappeared. And it would have happened the fall when Dustin was nine and we were in Miss Tyleson's third-grade class. I closed my eyes and pictured Dustin kicking the leg of my desk yesterday, right after he'd told me his mother was gone.

One . . . two . . . three . . . four . . . five . . . six . . . seven . . . eight . . . nine.

I looked at the jumble of clothes on my floor from this morning, when I'd been trying to put together writerly outfits. It seemed like a month ago. I dug through things until I found my poetry journal, and I opened it to a clean page.

Earbug, I wrote carefully for a title, and started a new poem.

Late the next afternoon I was up in the hayloft, still working on *Earbug,* when Luke called from right below me, "Carly, are you up there or something?"

I sighed. "Yes, Luke. Come on up, but be careful on the ladder."

Luke loved the hayloft, but he wasn't allowed up in it unless somebody was with him, which meant you hardly ever had privacy. I heard some excited little grunts as he climbed the wide-apart rungs of the rough wooden ladder, then he appeared in the square opening in the floor and came skidding over to kneel beside me in the hay.

"Careful! Don't run when you're up here, Lukey." I took his elbow and eased him down so we were sitting together on the floor with our legs dangling out the window and one of my arms around his waist. "From now on this is going to be my writing studio," I explained.

"Wow!" he whispered, impressed.

"We writers prefer solitude," I explained to him. "Our friends may misunderstand us, but we take solace in our art."

"What's solacetude and all those other yucky words?" Luke asked, like I was afraid he might.

Just then, an obnoxious grinding sound started up below us.

"Carly, look!" Luke yelled, pointing outside.

An oily shadow was spreading up the long lane to our house. I squinted, and the shadow became the Groats' junky flatbed truck, enclosed in a thick purple cloud of exhaust fumes.

My heart slammed, and I scooted back from the window, dragging Luke with me. What if they were here because they'd seen Noah and me spying on their compound yesterday morning?

"Carly, let me loose before I bite!" Luke whined, trying to wriggle out of my grip.

I held him harder. "Luke, be *quiet!* I *mean* it! We can't let them see us!"

Something in my voice got through to him, and he didn't squirm or make a peep again till the truck was nearly to the top of our lane. Then: "That's that truck with the skeleton on the front!" he whispered excitedly.

The Groats' truck was tattooed, like the Groats themselves. There was a pirate skull and crossbones painted on the hood. For the first time, I noticed they flew a small Rebel flag from their radio antenna. Eight men were sitting in back along the edges of the truck bed, their legs dangling loosely. They all wore black boots with little chains on them, not brown lace-up work boots like my dad and the other farmers wore.

The two men up front in the cab had shoulder-length greasy hair held out of their eyes by leather bands across their foreheads. They looked like if they ever smiled it would be a making-fun-of-you smile. They also seemed sweatier than real people, and one of them wore a black vest with no shirt beneath it.

The truck stopped with a clattering hiss in the driveway right below us, and I scrambled to a chink in the hayloft wall and stared down.

"What can I do for you?" I heard my father call from the part of the barn where the combine is usually parked.

"Come to talk about cutting your wood," the man driving yell-growled back. He leaned out his window and spit something big into the dirt.

All the men dropped from the truck and followed Daddy's voice into the barn. A wave of relief went

55

through me, followed by a ripple of disappointment. They weren't here to accuse Noah and me of spying, thank goodness. But I wasn't going to be close enough to hear their conversation.

The last thing I saw as they disappeared into the barn was one of the men running a big knife under his fingernails. A *big* knife, like Mom uses to scrape out the insides of dead chickens.

Luke crept up and squatted near the window again, peering down at the truck. I crouched beside him and put my arm back around his waist. "Careful. Don't go so near the edge. Those people are the Groats. You can see from how they spit and have all those tattoos that they're kind of . . . mean. That's why we had to hide from them."

Luke got wide-eyed. "Look, down on the truck! It's a Goatboy!"

Sure enough, Dustin was on the truck bed, crawling through the messy, mud-brown tangle of ropes and tools that at first had camouflaged him. As Luke and I watched, he hung from the side of the truck like a clump of mud, then dropped, like the men had.

"A Groat boy," I corrected Luke, whispering. "That's Dustin Groat. He's in my class at school."

I expected Dustin to follow the men into the barn, but he just stood there alone, staring at the ground with his hands on his hips, kicking the dust.

And then he began talking to himself again. This time I was too far away to hear, but I could see his mouth moving, and he kept kicking the truck tire with his heavy boot to emphasize his words.

After a few minutes, Dustin's gross relatives came back out and swarmed like a dark shadow over their truck. The truck moved in its sputtering way down our hill and finally disappeared from our lane like a nightmare disappears when you wake up.

Luke slumped against me. I felt myself go limp, too.

"Tell me a story about that Goatboy, okay?" Luke whispered.

I didn't bother telling him again it was a Groat boy, not a Goatboy. It's hard to explain, but suddenly I needed the comfort of make-believe, too.

I squinted toward the purplish smudge that was Kosh Woods, disappearing into the twilight. Out there in the true darkness of the thick trees, coyotes began howling.

"Well, once there was this kicking Goatboy. He was half-goat, half-boy, but he looked almost all boy. He walked on two feet, and his jeans hid his tail and furry legs. He also had horns on his head, but they were tiny."

"So his scraggly hair covered his horns and people couldn't see?"

"Right, his hair covered them. The Goatboy lived where the muddy river edged up against the Enchanted Woods. And, uh, besides the Goatboy, there were three gorgeous dancing fairies in the Enchanted Woods, and their names were Randiandella, Alicianna, and Caralotta the Beautiful." I swallowed. "And . . . Caralotta was the best dancer because she was the most beautiful and graceful of the three."

Luke raised his head and looked at me with his eyes narrowed impatiently, so I hurried to the part he was waiting for. "And, of course, there was the handsome prince who lived in the castle tower of the Enchanted Woods, Lucas the Magnificent. He ruled everybody and everything. He wouldn't let the Goatboy be obnoxious to the dancing fairies. He wouldn't let him head butt them on the slide, or cuss, or spit on their dancing slippers. Or on their table in school."

"Why?" Luke asked, settling his head against my shoulder.

"Because it's not nice to head butt, or to spit."

"I mean, why did the Goatboy be not nice?" he murmured, then yawned.

I shrugged. "How should I know?"

"Because you're telling the story!"

I sighed. "He was not nice because he wanted to be not nice. He was what you call a nemesis, which is someone who does what they want to when they want to, period."

I paused, and Luke didn't say anything. His head sagged against my shoulder in this heavy, sweaty way that told me he was probably asleep.

nine

When I came down to breakfast the next morning, Luke was waiting with an important presidential update.

"George Washington was the father of our free country, Carly!" he announced.

"Actually, Lucas, you already mentioned that last week," I told him, smiling in a sophisticated way. This morning I'd quickly created a poetic outfit using everything black I owned. I'd also put a little bath powder on my face—I knew poets looked pale and dramatic, like writing took a lot out of you.

"No, Carly, our *free* country! Our democracy! We just learned that democracy part Friday."

Mom walked over with eggs and put her hand on my forehead. "You look washed out, Carly. You okay?"

"Of course, Mother."

Noah was out on the kitchen porch, hanging up his milking overalls. He came through the door, yanked my hair as usual, and said, "Hey, Carl, whose funeral?"

I started to roll my eyes, then realized a writer wouldn't do that. "I won't eleviate your remark with a comment," I informed him, calmly spooning my grapefruit. I realized one second too late I meant "elevate," not "eleviate," but Noah had straddled his chair and was too busy shoveling all the plates of food toward himself to notice.

"George Washington was the father of our free country, Noah!"

"You got that right, kid," Noah agreed through a mouthful of eggs.

"You are wearing an awful lot of black, Carly," Mom said. "Pretty dreary for a beautiful fall day like this one."

I bounced my chair a little farther under the table, hoping no one would notice the color of my tights. "I'm sure in New York City and San Francisco all the cool, artistic people wear black from head to toe every single day," I informed them. "I'll bet only in the Midwest do people wear bright, glaring colors. My theory is that we copy animals out here."

A big squirt of grapefruit juice picked that second to ricochet off my spoon, hitting my eye. I yelped and ran to get a wet paper towel, and Noah laughed.

"Oh, yeah, Carl, you are just *so* cool!"

I turned on the faucet, keeping my back to them. I

looked out the big window over the sink and was surprised to see Daddy just standing out there in the yard, looking off toward Kosh Woods with his hands in his pockets and a sad expression on his face.

Mom stepped beside me and put her arm around my shoulders.

"He's upset because yesterday Sol Groat and his brothers came out here to ask him a favor, and he had to say no," she said softly. "The last few years he's let the Groats cut wood on our land, but there comes a time when you just can't take that kind of chance, with everyone so lawsuit-happy these days. And it seems that family gets more . . . unpredictable all the time."

"Daddy likes to help people," I said.

She put her cheek against my hair. "I think most people try to help each other," she murmured. "If you can give a person a chance to do something worthwhile, it might keep them from doing something . . . different."

As I waited for the bus at the bottom of our hill that morning, my brain touched the awful argument Randi and Ali and I had been having, like you'd touch a sore tooth with your tongue.

"I'm sitting by you on the bus today," I informed Luke.

"It's a free country!" he piped, grinning.

Two helicopters were going over. I shaded my eyes with my hand and followed their eerie black shadows across the bright fields.

Noah was squinting at them, too. "Everybody says the state police are sending those helicopters out to look for that methamphetamine lab over at the Groats'."

"There comes the bus," Luke announced, and my stomach did a flip-flop. Even sitting up front with Bryce and Luke, it would be tricky ignoring Alicia and Randi, who would surely be glaring at my back.

I didn't want to sit beside Randi and Alicia in class that morning, so I took the only empty desk, the back-row one I'd used to interview Dustin from the week before. As I walked toward it, Jasmine leaned into the aisle and whispered, "What happened to your real clothes?"

Some other girls were staring up at me too, waiting to hear my answer. What did they think, that I'd fallen in the mud and been dressed by the nurse in spare clothes, like a kindergartener? I just shrugged and went on down the aisle. How can you explain artistic sophistication to regular people, especially in five seconds?

"All right, class, please *stand* and move your desks to interview position!" Ms. Aspen called out as soon as roll and lunch count were taken that morning. Everybody stayed in their seats and heaved themselves and their desks around together. Ms. Aspen put her hands over her ears.

I lugged my desk around so it faced the back corner, then walked it the few feet to Dustin. When I heard the metallic thud of the front of my desk hitting his, it suddenly occurred to me that he might get the wrong idea about me moving closer to him.

"By the way, I didn't want to move back here," I told him, flipping nervously through the pages of my notebook, thinking fast. "I had to, because, uh, my eyesight is sort of blurry and my mother thinks one of my eyes is going bad and I've got to test it this week from the back of the room."

"Who hit you?" Dustin asked.

"Huh?" He'd caught me off-guard with that shocking question.

"Somebody gave you a smack in the left eye, but looks like they pulled their punch in time not to bruise it much. Who gave you that bad eye, your father? And then your mother tried to cover it up with goop?"

My father? I carefully touched my eye and felt a slick, unpowdered place under it where the grapefruit juice had hit at breakfast. "I . . . uh, I mean . . . nobody . . . uh . . ."

Never in my whole entire life had the possibility of anyone hitting me crossed my mind. And the thought of my father, of all people . . . I just suddenly couldn't get ahold of words to express how sickening that idea was.

While I floundered, Dustin gave a bored sigh and began staring down at his own right hand, which was hunched up into a little igloo shape at the corner of his desk.

I took several deep breaths, then finally got out,

"Do . . . do you want to interview me today?" hoping with all my heart he would say no.

Ignoring my question, Dustin lowered his chin to his desk. He cracked open a tiny sliver of space between the thumb and index finger of his igloo hand, and squinted into it.

Suddenly, he slapped his palm down so hard I jumped. Something that had been flattened between his palm and the desk began buzzing loudly and angrily.

I clamped my hands over my mouth as Dustin slowly peeled his hand from the desk. A huge blue fly was stuck to the middle of his palm by its own squished insides. It was still slightly alive, but buzzing now in only a halfhearted way.

I couldn't stop staring. With that smashed fly still weakly wriggling on his palm, Dustin poked himself in the chest with his left thumb. And suddenly, sickeningly, the left side of his shirt began moving, squirming all around, like there was some weird growth under there.

"Got your favorite breakfast for you," Dustin murmured to his chest.

I didn't dare breathe as Dustin carefully opened his shirt pocket a tiny crack and dropped the weakly writhing fly inside. His shirt moved wildly for a few seconds, then finally was still.

Dustin leaned forward slowly, holding his pocket

open so that I had to either clamp my eyes shut or take a look.

I braced myself and took a look. Deep inside, in a neat little nest of grass and clover, was an adorable, tiny, pure-white and slippery-looking frog. It stared up at me with reddish eyes, its throat throbbing.

After a few seconds, Dustin picked up a gum wrapper that was lying on the floor and began tearing it into small strips. He tucked those strips, one at a time, carefully into his pocket, making his frog a soft little bed.

ten

When Ms. Aspen dismissed us to go to music class later that morning, I waited till Ali and Randi had gone on, then I walked with Leigh Ann. When I got sick of her staring at my outfit, I said I'd forgotten something and dropped back to walk with Jasmine.

"You've got something weird on your face," Jasmine told me, so I ducked into the rest room and washed off what was left of the white bath powder. This made me a couple of minutes late, but it didn't matter because everyone was up and milling around Mr. Norville's room when I finally got there.

Mr. Norville had been telling us all fall that he'd check out recorders to us, and now he was actually doing it. As people crowded around his desk, he marked down names in his grade book before handing each person a little wooden flute, snug in a felt case.

"We'll be playing two or three recorder pieces for the Maple Leaf assembly next month, so everyone practice hard on what we're learning in class. Remember, these are real musical instruments, not toys! This is a special privilege, reserved for sixth graders because of your mature sense of responsibility."

It was nearly impossible to hear him, since everybody was already practicing.

"Peo-ple," Mr. Norville pleaded in a way he himself might have called double forte, "listen up!"

The recorder honking petered out.

"Thank you." Mr. Norville stood up and took out his handkerchief. He wiped his face and then the top of his head.

He paused. "Any questions?" he asked, then raised his black eyebrows and hunched his shoulders like he was expecting the worst.

Eric Gilman shot up his hand. "Mr. Norville, can I play electric guitar instead?"

Dustin was looking at his recorder, carefully placing his fingers over the holes as his shirt pocket thumped and jiggled. He was holding his left elbow against his side in this stiff sort of way.

"Why do you keep looking over at Dustin Groat?" Jasmine whispered, wrinkling her nose.

"I don't!" I informed her, wrinkling my nose right back.

But it was impossible to get my mind off Dustin and that awful question: *Who gave you that bad eye, your father?*

I ate lunch that day with the Harwood twins, Junie and Janis, then went with them out to the schoolyard for recess. But while they leaned against the bike racks, kissing pictures of hunky guys in a movie magazine, I quickly looked around the schoolyard for Dustin. He wasn't out there. Out of loyalty to Randi and Ali, even though we were fighting, shouldn't I have gone into the gym where they were practicing jazz dancing to warn them that Dustin was probably under the bleachers, spying on them? I *should* have warned them clear last Friday, when I'd caught him in the act. Why hadn't I?

My eyes settled on Joey Snyder. He and a bunch of his friends were chasing this poor little squirrel who was only trying to reach the safety of his oak tree. They were standing between the tree and the squirrel, waving sticks, playing keep-away with that confused animal so that he was trembling all over.

Dustin hadn't been spying last Friday, though. I'd pretty much known it all along, I guess, but suddenly I was sure of it.

Dustin had been hiding from Joey and the rest of us.

When I got home that afternoon, I peeled off my itchy and hot black clothes and kicked them into a tangle at the back of my closet. Writing was hard enough without being itchy and hot and having people stare at your powder, and life was complicated enough without worrying about coming up with black dye.

I put on jeans and headed up to my poetry studio. With my feet dangling from the hayloft window, I opened my notebook to *Earbug* and started some serious revising.

The poem I'd started the day Noah and I went to the river bottom was about a kid living in such a gross place that when his mother dies he starts sticking sharp things into his ears and knuckles and cussing and kicking and he eventually forgets how to act human and starts crawling instead of walking and gradually turns into a gigantic bug.

Now that seemed totally wrong—silly, in fact.

I bent over my notebook, writing and erasing and writing and erasing till my page was wrinkled and nearly transparent. When I finally looked back up, I felt disoriented. The light was grayer—more like early evening than late afternoon. A car was coming up our lane. The sound must have been what had brought me out of my writing trance.

I worked a few more minutes. Then, exhausted and hungry, I slung my poetry journal over my shoulder and climbed down the hayloft ladder.

I was starting out the barn door when I saw that Mr. and Mrs. Arnett, some neighbors from down the road, were sitting on our porch, talking to my parents.

"Well, it's a shame about those Groats, is what it is," I heard Mr. Arnett say.

I darted back inside the barn shadows and shoved my ear hard against an open knothole, holding my breath.

"A person would like to help them, but they'll turn it against you every time. Always have. Take Joe Lawson. Everybody knows what happened there. Out of the goodness of his heart he gives Jack Groat a job bucking bales, then Jack gets the idea it was Joe who told the police about their marijuana patch last year, and Joe's hay barn mysteriously burns to the ground one night. Or that teacher Sarge Groat took into his head to terrorize a few years back. She got so spooked by Sarge Groat she moved back to St. Louis in the middle of the year without so much as a fare-thee-well."

"Miss Tyleson," Mrs. Arnett said, nearly too softly for me to hear.

Miss Tyleson? She'd been my third-grade teacher, and I'd been wondering forever why she suddenly disappeared!

"They just lead such a vicious, careless life," Mrs. Arnett said, as though all the Groats were one big thing.

Explain about Miss Tyleson being terrorized!

"But when there are children involved, you want to do all you can," Mom said.

Mrs. Arnett sighed. "Oh, yes, when there are children involved, it breaks your heart."

"Well, Ron, I say you made the best decision," said Mr. Arnett. "The only decision. They've taken advantage of your good nature for too many years already."

I beat the barn wood with my fists in frustration. *Get back to Miss Tyleson!* But none of them said a single thing for several seconds.

70

"Well, I appreciate your concern, Henry," my father finally drawled, "but to tell you the honest truth, I somewhat regret telling them they couldn't cut wood out here this year. I truly got the impression that if I don't change my mind and give them permission to cut on our land and nobody else does either, they'll take to cutting illegally in Kosh Woods again, like they did three summers back. You remember that mess? Started with them just cutting wood, but ended with them taking over the woods that fall for drinking and carousing and even gunplay."

"And that led to tragedy," Mom said so softly that, again, I barely heard. "My heart still breaks for those poor, motherless children."

"Oh, yes," Mrs. Arnett echoed. "Tragedy, tragedy."

Tragedy? What kind of tragedy?! Why didn't they explain anything important!

"Well, they always hurt themselves worse than they hurt anybody else," Mr. Arnett pronounced, like a teacher would state a fact in class. "That's one good thing."

"Henry," Mrs. Arnett breathed in a soft, scolding way.

"Maybe I'll run into town in the morning and ask Mayor Casken to let them cut deadfall in Kosh Woods for just a few days," Daddy said. "You can never tell. It might satisfy them."

"Better to offer them something than to wait till they decide to just up and take everything, I guess," Mr. Arnett mumbled.

eleven

Noah had gone to an out-of-town soccer game, so when everyone else had gone on to bed that night I took a blanket and my pillow and settled in against his bedroom door to wait for him. I was asleep but came instantly awake when I finally heard him taking the stairs two at a time and clomping down the dark hallway.

"Hey, Noah? Why did Miss Tyleson move away?" I quickly whispered before he could step on me with his heavy cowboy boots.

"Whoa, Carl! Where . . . are you?"

"Down here. On the floor by your door."

"What're you doing down there?"

"Noah, pay attention! Mr. Arnett was over here this afternoon and he said that Sarge Groat scared Miss Tyleson out of town. Is that true?"

Noah snorted. "Mr. Arnett's always griping," he said, which I knew already but which didn't have much to do with my question. Noah dropped his jacket and folded himself down to sit on it and pull off his boots. "Miss Tyleson? That teacher that looked like a high school kid? She left in the middle of her first year here."

"Noah! I know—she was *my* teacher that year! Mr. Arnett said Sarge Groat terrorized her! Is that true?"

"Dunno. Could be. She always looked scared of everything when I saw her in the halls. She was so young and all." Noah yawned out loud, stretching his long arms over his head, then reaching them out sideways so his fingertips grazed the walls on each side of us. Suddenly he grinned. "I got the impression Miss Tyleson wasn't that great at class discipline. You were always coming home and talking about all this spitting and kicking and stuff that went on in your class, especially with Dustin. Remember when Dad got sick of you whining all the time that year and told you to try and walk in Dustin's shoes for a while? He told you that three or four times, Carl, and each time you turned green! You really took it literally."

"That never happened!" I informed him, though suddenly I remembered picturing my feet wriggling through slime as they slid into Dustin's cruddy shoes.

"And also, Noah, I didn't whine about him all the time."

Noah stood, shaking his head and still snickering. "Anything you say, Carl." He dragged his heavy jacket over my face as he went into his room and shut the door behind him.

An hour later, I was still lying awake, staring out my window at the jagged black fringe Kosh Woods made along the bottom of the night sky. Something big had happened the fall we were in third grade. Something that had started with the Groats' cutting wood illegally and had ended with . . . what? Did it have something to do with Dustin's mother dying? And how was it all connected to Miss Tyleson?

When our desks were nose to nose for interview time the next morning, I realized it would take tons of nerve to ask Dustin what I really wanted to know.

"Tell me about your . . ." *Just ask him! About his mother! How she died!*

I glanced up. Dustin's shirt pocket bulged a little— a warm, alive-looking bulge. He had his recorder in its felt case balanced on the pencil slot on his desk. He reached forward and touched it with the fingertips of his left hand, as if he got some kind of comfort from it.

Something about that made me chicken out.

". . . father," I finished weakly. "Who is your father?"

"Sarge Groat," Dustin mumbled. "You were staring down at his knife when we were out to your place last Sunday, remember?"

"You . . . saw me?" My voice sounded wheezy and far away. "Up in the hayloft?"

His chin was pointed downward so far it nearly rested on his chest, but for once he raised his eyes and looked directly at me. I saw him swallow, twice. Two long swallows.

"Is that where you go to hide from your father?" he asked.

"What?" I whispered, my ears ringing.

He squeezed his recorder case with both hands, and his eyelids quivered slightly. "Is that where you hide?" he repeated. "When they're after you? Do your brothers hide there, too?"

"I . . . we . . . uh . . . it's just where I go," I said.

He put his elbows on his desk and leaned toward me. He began turning that safety pin in his knuckle, and this time he didn't grimace with the pain or even seem to notice that he was doing it.

"I got this tunnel," he said in a rush. "Starts a tunnel, joins up into a cave. They don't follow. It's partly collapsed is why. Too close on the sides for them."

"Who?" I whispered.

"Nobody," he answered. "I told you—don't nobody follow. Leads to the woods from under the floor in one of our sheds."

"Koshkanong Woods?"

"Desperadoes dug it for escape, way back in olden times."

"But . . . who? Who doesn't follow you?"

Dustin hunched his left shoulder up against his left ear and winced, then put his head down on his desk and closed his eyes.

"Them," he mumbled.

My blood was surging against my eardrums, making a wavelike sound that I at first thought was getting so loud my head must be exploding. Then I noticed there were helicopters in the window, flying low and making so much noise that everyone had stopped interviewing to watch them as they barely cleared the swings and slides on the schoolyard.

Dustin turned his head toward the window and listlessly watched them, too.

The sky seemed like the blue paper sky Mr. Norville used as a backdrop for school plays. The shiny helicopters looked like huge flying bugs about to rip right through it.

Nothing seemed real.

Sitting between the Harwood twins in the cafeteria that day, I watched as Dustin took a banana and a piece of something flat and brown from his lunch sack. That sack looked wrinkled and greasy in every possible place, like he'd used it forever.

Is that where you hide when they're after you? That sentence wouldn't quit creeping into my head, and each time it did, I felt sick inside.

Dustin yanked big animal-like bites from the flat

brown stuff and chewed it open-mouthed. He was straddling the end of one of the benches near the corner, his back to as many people as possible.

What does Dustin think about? I wondered as I watched Adam Gerber run over to peer into Dustin's ear, then run away, laughing.

I guess I didn't really realize I'd said anything out loud, till I heard Junie answer my question. "My dad says those Groats spend all their time thinking about what they can get away with next," she said.

twelve

On the bus that afternoon, Bryce leaned across me to Luke.

"Is she gonna sit with us forever?" he whined.

"I cannot tell a lie," Luke answered. "I sure, sure, sure *hope* not."

Suddenly, Randi appeared in the aisle right next to us.

"So, Carly, are you, you know, still mad?" she asked.

Randi and Ali and I have never had a fight that lasted more than two or three days. I'd meant to stay mad forever this time, but I just couldn't keep it up. I guess they must have had that happen, too.

I wet my lips. "Are you?" I asked back.

"No," Randi said.

"Neither am I," I told her with a shrug and a smile.

I stood and began squeezing out of Luke and Bryce's seat. "Hate to break your hearts, guys, but I've gotta go."

"It won't break *my* heart," Bryce said solemnly. "I'll be *glad*."

"Sorry I was so grouchy in the gym Friday," I admitted to Randi and Ali when we were settled in our usual bus seat. "I guess I was just, you know . . . embarrassed in front of the basketball boys. I mean, you guys are good dancers, but, well, I don't know about me. I mean, I'm not a gymnast, and I don't have all that much . . . attitude and stuff."

I was kind of hoping they'd tell me I *was* good, which they didn't. But Randi said, "We're sorry, too, for leaving you out when we changed the interviews. Everybody just takes for granted that because you're smart you want to do assignments the hard way."

I smiled. I was pretty sure that was a compliment.

"And we have an idea!" Randi leaned toward me excitedly. "You know how Todd and Cassie have been interviewing each other? Well, they broke up yesterday, and now Todd said he'd rather interview anybody, even Dustin, than her, so you can interview Cassie!"

Alicia nodded enthusiastically.

"But . . . we've been interviewing for four days already. Ms. Aspen surely won't let anybody switch now."

I was sure she wouldn't have let anybody switch in the first place if she'd known about it, but I didn't mention that.

Randi just shrugged lightly. "Everybody's moving around so much that she doesn't have any idea of who's got who. And haven't you noticed that she uses our interview time to finish filling out the lunch count and stuff? She's not even paying attention."

Alicia offered me a Lifesaver. Pineapple, my favorite, was on top, and I took it and started sucking. Some muscles deep in my jaws puckered up and throbbed for a second, and my eyes got watery, reacting to the tartness.

"Ali, remember when we were all talking at lunch the day I first drew Dustin to interview? You said Dustin was too quiet now to call obnoxious. Well, can you remember exactly when he started gradually changing from being obnoxious to being too quiet?"

Alicia shrugged. "In Miss Tyleson's class, I'm pretty sure."

"But he didn't gradually change," Randi blurted. "I remember that perfectly. One day he was driving everybody crazy, Carl—especially you, of course. And the next day he just plopped down in the back row and started staring at his desk or his stomach or whatever like a lobotomized zombie. Like Frankenstein's monster. And he's been like that ever since."

"What do you mean, 'of course,' Randi? He didn't drive me any crazier than anybody else!" I knew I should be more polite, especially since we were barely back to not being mad. But why did she have to say anything that popped into her head, true or not?

She shrugged. "I just meant, Carl, that you were the smartest one in our class, and Dustin was the dumbest one, so of course everybody understood why he drove you crazier than the rest of us." She began finger-combing her hair back. "Anyhow, Dustin isn't your project any longer, so it doesn't even matter. You'll definitely get editor interviewing Cassie."

It was getting hard to swallow the pineapple juice from the Lifesaver.

"Thanks for offering me Cassie, you guys," I heard myself say, "but I think I'll just keep Dustin."

I knew I shouldn't let Randi's warped memory of how things were three entire long years ago get me down, but all that afternoon as I helped Mom husk and freeze corn, I just couldn't quit thinking about it. Why did Randi have so many off-the-wall opinions this year, anyway? Dustin had driven everybody *equally* crazy in Miss Tyleson's class! *Everybody!* Period.

"Penny for your thoughts," Mom said. "You're awfully quiet."

I shrugged. "Nothing to say," I murmured.

Up in my room after dinner and dishes, I sprawled on my stomach across my bed, reading the poem I'd worked so hard on in the hayloft the day before.

81

Earbug

I am less important than an earbug to you,
And so, like a bug, I have to hide.
You force me into my own cocoon
Because I think you'll squish me if I step outside.
I am less important than a frog to you,
And so, like a pocket frog, I keep out of sight.
But deep inside this dark place, if you only knew,

". . . if you only knew," I repeated, whispering. The last line was definitely going to be the hard one.

Sighing, I closed my notebook, flopped onto my back, and stared at the ceiling. Moths were bonking into the overhead light, so I got up and turned it off, then went to the window and knelt, looking out.

There were so many stars and so many fireflies, it was impossible to tell which was which. "Tragedy, tragedy," I whispered to the puckery old purple-faced moon.

"Carl, you talking to me?"

I gasped. "Nuh . . . Noah, is that you? Where . . . are you?"

"Out here, on the roof under my window."

I unhooked my screen and stuck my head out. Sure enough, I could barely see a shadow that was him, perched on the steep porch roof like one of those gargoyles they have on ancient cathedrals. I knew he sometimes sneaked out through his window, using the trellis along the side of the porch as a ladder to the ground, but I'd never seen him just *balancing* on the roof like this.

"Be careful!" I whispered. It was pretty obvious he was thinking about Julie under this black and starry sky. He was staring toward the part of Kosh Woods you couldn't see from the ground, the part that edged up against the river bottom.

It was so, so romantic, and so, so sad.

"Maybe you should just, you know . . . drive by there again," I whispered. "I mean, maybe if Julie saw you she'd sneak out and meet you or something."

I heard him take in a deep breath and let it out. "Where do you think I've been the last two nights?" he mumbled. "Sunday night, when I told the folks I was studying with Steve, I drove out there; then I went again after the game last night. Last night I had to swerve into the ditch to keep from hitting one of their pigs in the road. When it squealed, someone behind that fence of theirs took a shot at the truck."

"Noah! They actually . . ."

"Y'know, it's not like I want some huge thing," he went on, as if he hadn't heard me. "I mean, I know it wouldn't work out for us. I just want to see her one time to find out how she is, you know? To find out if she's, well, okay."

"Oh, Noah, promise you won't go over there again! They actually took a shot at you?"

"At the truck," he mumbled. "Guess they're jumpy

because of that methamphetamine lab and those helicopters. The police are flying over there all the time, Carl. Even at night. That must be some lab."

"Or maybe there's something else even *worse* out there," I said, not exactly sure what I meant by that, but shivering anyway. "You should have heard our folks and the Arnetts yesterday, Noah. They kept talking about the Groats, about carousing and gunplay, and then Mom said it all led to tragedy. And that stuff was connected somehow to Miss Tyleson, so I know it happened three years ago, but Daddy made it sound like the same thing could happen again this fall. It was so creepy, listening to them. I wish I knew what *happened* exactly. You said Dustin's mother drowned, but *how'd* she drown, Noah? I mean, why? Was she trying to save someone? Was she lost in the dark? Just how?"

"Lots of people have drowned in the swamp, Carl," Noah said. "Back in Civil War days, five Groat women drowned out there in one single night. They'd been to some battlefield, tending to their sons and husbands who'd been wounded riding with Quantrill's Raiders. And coming home they were so exhausted and upset they just lost their bearings and fell in. That's how the story goes, anyhow. You're supposed to be able to still hear their moans on clear winter nights."

"The moans of the . . . swamp fiends, right?"

Noah laughed, but he sounded a million miles away. "Yeah, well, all those old stories people tell started with truth and just sort of got out of hand, I guess."

I saw his shadow heeling itself up so it was sitting on his windowsill. "I'm going in, Carl," he said listlessly. "Don't let the swamp boogies sneak into your room."

But just as he started to swing his legs around, we both heard music coming from Kosh Woods. I caught my breath and strained forward, and Noah froze, straddling the windowsill, one leg in his room and one leg out.

It wasn't twangy country music, like from someone's truck radio. It wasn't thumping rock music, like from Randi's tape player. It was living music—simple, eerie, and sad. Mostly scales and trills. Recorder music!

thirteen

Sounds like somebody's playing one of those things Mr. Norville makes you mess with in sixth grade so you'll know if you want to be in junior high band," Noah murmured. "And whoever's playing it sure knows what he's doing more than anybody in *my* class did." He faced me in the darkness. "Can anybody in sixth grade this year play that well?"

"Mr. Norville only checked the recorders out to us a couple of days ago," I told him, thinking of the protective way Dustin held his. "And no one my age could be out in Kosh Woods at night." *No one with a mother to stop them, that is.*

Noah shrugged. "Strange," he said, then swiveled his other leg into his room.

"Noah, wait! Tell me the truth. I know you didn't

mean to, but you really got me worried last night when you said I used to whine all the time about Dustin."

I waited for him to tell me he'd just been teasing, but Noah didn't say anything.

"I mean, everybody was *equally* grossed out by him in third grade. How were *we* supposed to know his mother had just died?" But come to think of it, why hadn't we known? Why hadn't our teachers and parents told us about it?

"So, what do you want me to tell you the truth about, Carl?" Noah asked.

I swallowed. "Nothing, I guess," I said. "G'night, Noah."

" 'Night, Carl." He disappeared into his room, and I heard his window scrape closed.

Still I stood in my own open window, listening to the music. My throat ached like it had earlier on the bus.

I pushed my window open wider, and before I really knew I was doing it, I scrambled out onto my own section of porch roof. *Don't look down!* I ordered myself as I edged along the shingles. When I reached the trellis, I groped with my feet for the first rung, then I half-climbed, half- slid quickly to the ground.

You can't do this, Carly! I told myself as I stumbled through the side yard, but when I reached the moonlit soybean field, I slid into its golden waves like a person slipping her skin. It's hard to explain, but I felt, then, like someone else, not like someone whose parents would kill her if they caught her doing what she was doing.

Kosh Woods was barely visible ahead of me, slightly darker than the sky. I finally reached its edge and stopped with my hands on my knees, gulping air, listening. *Yes!* There was that mysterious music still, coming from the part of the woods where several huge old oak trees grew beside the big bend in Koshkanong Creek.

I ran on tiptoe into the trees and toward the music. The woods at first seemed pitch dark, but my ears and skin felt totally alert. I imagined myself avoiding the trees and vines and snarls of wild, thorny plants the same way the coyotes and other wild animals do, by a sort of skin radar.

My eyes adjusted to the darkness, and I saw huge Chandler's Oak, the tallest tree in Kosh Woods, ahead and to my left, its ancient limbs like a fat woman's arms reaching up to lazily fluff out her hair. The creek was a dark, living thing, a sparkling snake slipping along beside the tree's long roots.

Now the music was coming from very nearby. I slowed to a stealthy creep—bending forward, holding my breath, and listening.

Suddenly a glowing giant's eye peered across the dense ground cover at me.

My heart slammed and I barely stifled a scream before I realized it was lamplight pouring from a shallow slit in the limestone bank of the creek.

This must be the mouth of the tunnelly cave Dustin

had told me about, the one he used as an escape route! The opening in the stone was no more than a foot high and maybe three feet wide. Anyone passing it would have assumed it was just a hollowed ledge of rock, a good home for water snakes.

Squinting, I could begin to see a black silhouette crouched just outside that lamplit opening. Dustin! He was wiping his recorder on his shirttail.

I came a couple of careful steps closer and hid behind a snarl of wild blackberry vines. The lamplight reflected off something at Dustin's feet, something so bright and white that at first I thought it might be a diamond he'd mined from that lost tunnel.

I squinted harder. It was his tiny frog, patiently sitting on a rock.

The wind came up out of nowhere like a warning. The lady tree made a "Whoo-woo" sound and seemed to be turning in all directions, looking for intruders.

Dustin jerked up his head.

The lamplight hit his face. His skin shone as brightly as his frog's, and he looked . . . different. Open, instead of closed. Unguarded in a way he never looked at school, as if out here, where everybody else was afraid to be, he didn't expect anything to hurt him.

I staggered a few steps backward. A vine grabbed my ankle, but I kicked free and turned away from Dustin's lamplight and into the deep darkness.

Trespasser, trespasser, trespasser! the leaves and locusts seemed to hiss together as I ran all the way home.

fourteen

Dustin wasn't at school the next day, which wasn't that unusual. He missed about a day a week, sometimes two or three.

Ms. Aspen didn't give us interview time that morning anyway, because Wednesday is our library morning. I thought I was going to check out a book, but instead I ended up looking through the Q encyclopedia for Quantrill's Raiders, those guys Noah said the Groats rode with in the Civil War. I was kind of surprised when I found it, or, I should say, them.

One of the most notorious, and possibly the bloodiest, of the guerrilla bands that fought in the name of the Confederacy during the Civil War was led by one William Quantrill. At various times, such postwar outlaws as Bloody Bill Anderson, Cole Younger, and Frank and Jesse James were numbered among the hundreds of roughriders who joined Quantrill in his raids to pillage and burn the towns of northwestern Missouri and eastern Kansas considered to be sympathetic to the Union cause.

I slid down to the floor and braced the book on my knees, fascinated.

Most historians believe Quantrill fought more to avenge private grudges than to uphold the Confederate cause, and no gruesome tactic seemed beyond his scope, including the cold-blooded killing of women and children. On several occasions, Quantrill and his raiders were reported to have burned entire families alive inside . . .

"Carly, your class is leaving." Mr. Hankins, our librarian, laughed at the way I'd jumped. "Sorry! Didn't mean to scare you."

I scrambled to my feet. "Mr. Hankins, could I keep this encyclopedia for a little while, please?"

He made a move to read over my shoulder. "My, what's so fascinating?"

I slammed the encyclopedia closed. Real person or not, this Quantrill was so sleazy the teachers might think reading about him was like watching a horror movie or something.

"Have it back by afternoon, Carly," Mr. Hankins said.

After lunch, Randi wanted to show us this new way of braiding hair that her cousin from St. Louis had explained to her over the phone. "Let's all go to the rest room and I'll braid everybody."

I walked with her, Alicia, Krista, and Jasmine as far as the cafeteria entrance. "You guys go on," I told them. "I have to take back this encyclopedia and I want to finish what I was reading first."

When they were safely around the corner, I headed for the gym. It was completely deserted and as magical as I remembered it being that dance practice day, before the basketball boys came thundering in and changed it.

I tiptoed to the edge of the bleachers, then crept into the shadowy gloom below them, into Dustin's realm. Beneath me the floor was sticky with leaked basketball-game drinks, and over my head the dim bleachers slanted down stepwise, so I felt like I was in a mysterious and ancient pyramid. I picked a not-too-sticky spot on the floor where a sliver of sun leaked down between two bleachers, and I settled in to refind my place in the encyclopedia.

. . . killing of women and children. On several occasions, Quantrill and his raiders were reported to have burned entire families alive inside their houses. The Confederacy never fully endorsed his tactics, and Quantrill belonged to no organized regiment. His appeal was mainly to the discouraged and disgruntled who felt themselves to be outsiders, victims of forces beyond their control.

I was rereading that last sentence when the gym door near the stage burst open and the basketball boys poured in, shaking the floor beneath me to what felt like about an 8.8 on the Richter scale. I closed the encyclopedia, trapping Quantrill inside.

It was a struggle pulling myself away from burning buildings and screaming children and back into the smelly, humid everydayness of the gym.

In fact, most of that afternoon I caught my attention wandering in class and realized I'd been watching a movie in my mind of these really sweaty, grim-faced guys riding fast and hard through the tall prairie grass west of Cooper's Glade. They were following the Confederate flag, giving out Rebel war whoops, raising guns over their heads and punching the air with them.

Sometimes in my brain movie they were riding horses, but other times they were on motorcycles.

When I went to the library to give back the encyclopedia at the end of the day, Mr. Hankins was waiting for me.

"Surprise, surprise, Carly!" He reached under the big checkout desk and whipped out an envelope. "When I saw how interested you are in the colorful vigilante history of our part of the state, I just happened to remember an article that ran in one of the Kansas City newspapers a couple of years ago. We luckily had it on microfiche, so I made you a copy. Enjoy! And remember, history *lives!*"

Actually, what I was remembering was that Mr. Hankins is our librarian two days a week, but in his other life he teaches history in the high school. Noah says he has a reputation for being one of those teachers who goes berserk when anyone acts the tiniest bit interested in his class.

"Thanks, Mr. Hankins," I said, trying to sound grateful enough. I figured the envelope contained a long, boring article that would strain your brain, so I stuck it in my notebook to try and read when I got home.

But the article turned out to be short—two paragraphs. The first one was scary and fascinating, and I read it three times.

For over a century and a quarter, no one knew the whereabouts of the remains of notorious Civil War renegade William Quantrill, killed in battle in 1865. Then just recently, a box containing Quantrill's headless skeleton was discovered in a closet in a Kansas museum. Kansas, the state which suffered the most from

Quantrill's deadly raids, shipped the remains immediately and unceremoniously back to Missouri, where they were finally laid to rest at the Confederate Cemetery at Higginsville.

Higginsville was only about an hour from here!
The second paragraph was even more fascinating, though not as juicy. I read it three times, too, then stuck it into the interview-question page of my notebook.

Hundreds of men from the northwestern part of Missouri rode with William Quantrill in the early 1860s, and after the war, many of them gave shelter and support to the outlaw gangs of Frank and Jesse James and the Younger brothers. Several area homeowners to this day, in fact, have been surprised to discover tunnels beneath their property, dug during long-gone vigilante days to provide gang members an escape route to nearby woods should suspicious lawmen appear.

fifteen

That night after dinner I went to practice my recorder in my hayloft poetry studio. Luke followed me up there and sat with his hands over his ears as I made it slowly through my scales.

"You're not that good," he informed me when I finished.

"Thank you very much for the brutal honesty, George Washington," I told him, but my feelings weren't hurt. After all, it was only my third day of practicing.

Then we both just sat and listened to the fall sounds—the cooing of the birds, the combines humming, the trees rustling their brittle leaves. There was also the buzz of the Groats cutting wood. Daddy had gotten the town council to let them cut deadfall out in Kosh Woods, just like he'd told Mr. Arnett he'd try to do.

There was a little shift of light, and Luke and I

turned our heads together to watch the sun slide behind the tree line. Then suddenly we heard music coming from the woods.

Dustin was getting really good, really fast.

Luke faced me, round-eyed. "That's a mugician!" he whispered. "Carly, there's a mugician living in our woods!"

I didn't have the heart to make another simple thing complicated for Luke.

"You know," I whispered back to him, "that sounds like the Goatboy of the Enchanted Woods, all right, playing his magical wooden flute."

Luke leaned back into the hay and got the same dreamy look on his face he used to get when he was a toddler and I told him bedtime stories. I halfway expected him to stick his thumb in his mouth.

"So the Goatboy's a mugician?" he asked trustingly, eager to half believe any wild and fantastic thing I told him. "And he has a wooden flute? Is it like the one you play, only he plays it good and you play it bad?"

"No, it's not one bit like mine. It's much easier to play." Okay, I guess my feelings *were* getting a little hurt. "You know the wooden whistle Grandpa carved for you out of three pieces of elm wood? It's more like that."

"Tell other stuff about the Goatboy mugician, Carly. Not about head butting and kicking. Other stuff."

I took a deep breath and blew it out slowly, thinking. "Well, did I tell you he was born with a bug living in his shaggy ear? In fact, the bug is why he spent lots of time alone. So many people were sneaking around, peeking into his ear and then laughing at him that he got sick of it. Now he stays in a lonely corner of the Enchanted Woods, playing his magical wooden flute with only a trusty pocket frog as a companion. In fact, back when he was in third grade, the Goatboy learned how to become invisible. So now, alone in his corner, he sometimes just . . . disappears."

I expected Luke to ask about the pocket frog, but he said, "He mostly makes himself invisible when he has to hide from mean fairies."

"Who said the fairies were mean? The Goatboy was obnoxious to Randiandella, Alicianna, and especially to Caralotta the Beautiful, not the other way around. He spit on their dancing shoes, remember? He cussed and kicked."

"They must have been laughing at his ear or calling him smelly and that's what made him be not nice!" Luke insisted. "Lucas the Magnificent would never laugh at the Goatboy. Especially not at his funny, shaggy hair. So the Goatboy lets Lucas see him any time he wants to."

"Whatever you say, Luke," I murmured, shaking the hay from my recorder case. Why was I wasting my breath arguing? This was just a silly fairy tale.

"I wish it was those bedtime-story days again, Carly," Luke said, his voice husky with sleepiness. I shoved him aside and stretched out on the hay myself, then reached over and took hold of his ankle. I'd tried several times lately to remember how it felt to be Luke's age, thinking everything was simple and having to find out, thing by thing, that it wasn't.

I felt Luke's foot go limp and I sat up quickly, before I could doze off, too. "Hey, Lukey, wake up! Don't ever go to sleep up here in the hayloft. You could roll right out the window! Luke!" I jiggled and jerked his ankle, and he came groggily around.

"I'm awake, Carly!" he complained, pinwheeling his arms, trying to kick and swat me away.

Dustin was back in class the next morning. As I pulled my desk up to his for interview time, I remembered I had that paragraph from Mr. Hankins's article to show him, so I held my notebook by its spiral and shook the little microfiched square of paper out. "This is *so* fascinating," I said, handing the paragraph across to Dustin. "Your tunnel is sort of famous. At least the guys who probably dug it were."

"What's that?" he mumbled, looking at the paper from under his long eyelashes. He leaned over and squinted at it.

"Go on, take it and read it! My arm's getting tired," I urged, but he slouched back in his chair and shook his head.

"Just read it!" I told him. "It won't take two seconds!"

Dustin just shook his head once more, in the same stubborn way he always shook it when Ms. Aspen tried to get him to read or answer some question in class.

I couldn't decide whether to waste my breath telling him about the history of his stupid tunnel or not, since he was acting so obnoxious. But I finally decided anything was better than just sitting and watching him be stubborn.

"Okay, then, I'll tell you what it says." I sighed, hoping he could see how annoyed I was. "But first I better explain who William Quantrill was."

"He was a great hero of the war," Dustin immediately said without looking up. Wincing a little, he readjusted his left arm. "When they buried William Quantrill's bones out to the cemetery in Higginsville, my uncles and me went, to pay respects. My uncle Sol, he wore my great-great-uncle Pete's greys and carried his bayonet. Uncle Jack wanted to wear the other uniform, but it got all shot up at the Battle of Lexington, just like Great-great-uncle Seth did. Jack put it on, but it was stiff as tanned hide, with the blood. Jack couldn't even bend at the waist to sit down."

I swallowed. "So . . . were Quantrill's men the ones who dug the tunnel under your shed?"

Dustin shook his head. "Cole Younger done that. Him and one of his brothers and some of their gang. They was good friends of my great-granddad's. He was kilt with one of Cole's brothers, holdin' up one of them

100

trains that carried money the government of Yankee thieves stole from the South after the war. Great-granddad's hand was shot off and he bled to death coming home through the swamp. They was heroes, Great-granddad and them."

Someone knocked the coffee mug of sharpened pencils off the corner of Ms. Aspen's desk right then, and I let out a yelp, thinking Jesse James and the Younger brothers had just come riding into the room, guns blazing.

I glanced over my shoulder. Several people were looking at me. "Sorry," I whispered, then turned quickly back to Dustin.

My head was spinning. Now I knew what Mr. Hankins meant when he said that history lives. Listening to Dustin's view of things, so different from the way I'd been taught things were back then, I had this feeling that it wasn't only dead outlaws we had under our feet. Everything that had ever happened might still be kicking around somewhere, ready to trip us up.

On my interview-question page I wrote, *Who were some of your ancestors?*, and after it I started eagerly writing, as close to word for word as I could, the juicy things that Dustin had just told me.

"Now I got a question for you," Dustin said, right out of the blue. "Why'd you tell me that sentence wrong that day?"

"What?" I murmured, still writing.

"Back in Miss Tyleson's class. That reading sentence. You told me all the wrong words that day. How come you did that?"

I was right in the middle of taking a breath, writing the word outlaws, noticing that my left elbow itched, arching my right foot around the desk leg, and shaking my bangs from my eyes. All those things stopped.

I felt myself burning, my neck mostly, my forehead, my eyes.

"I . . . I didn't," I stammered, not looking directly at him. "I mean, I don't know what you're talking about."

I stood up. "I forgot. I have to go do something."

I hurried out the classroom door, too mortified to even worry about whether Ms. Aspen was going to stop me, which she didn't. A few yards down the hall, I walked right into Mr. Cahill's mop bucket. He tried to make me let him look at where I'd bonked my shin, but I said it was fine and then I ran the rest of the way to the rest room.

The rest room closest to our classroom was once used by the high school girls instead of us. When we took it over, Mr. Cahill gave it several layers of paint, trying to cover the graffiti the high school girls had lipsticked on the walls. But every single bit of that graffiti was still readable. The green paint just made it more secret and interesting.

I tried to block Dustin's question from my mind by reading and rereading one of those lipsticked messages—*Joshua T. is a major hunk!!* Joshua T. was probably as old as my dad now, more proof that the past wasn't gone but merely hidden beneath a few layers of, in this case, thin green paint.

Why'd you tell me that sentence wrong . . . ?

My eyes scrinched shut, and I clamped my hands at the sides of my head. I slid down with my back against the wall and was crouching there like that when Randi and Alicia came in looking for me a couple minutes later.

"Carly, what's going on? Are you sick? Ms. Aspen sent us to . . ."

I jumped up and rushed at them, grabbing their arms. "Randi, can Dustin read? Ali, can he? Quick, tell me!"

"Sure he can," Randi said. "Remember when Mr. Yarborough had us read aloud all the time? Dustin read like everybody else."

"But that was in second grade," I whispered, shaking my head. "He never read in Miss Tyleson's class. Did . . . did he?"

"You know how he was then, Carl." Randi shrugged. "Out of control. I think he *could* read, he just didn't ever follow along. And Miss Tyleson hardly ever called on him."

I tried to force air into my lungs. "Remember when I told him the wrong sentence that day she suddenly *did* call on him?"

Randi narrowed her eyes then bounced on her heels, laughing. "Oh, Carl, that was so hilarious! You nailed him! It was *so* funny!"

103

"No!"

Randi took a quick step back from me, her eyes wide. Alicia carefully reached out a hand and touched my shoulder.

"Uh, Carly? We don't know what's got you so upset, but if Dustin couldn't read he'd be in a special reading class."

I couldn't talk, but I hugged my arms and started nodding, hoping with all my heart that Alicia's reasoning was not just precise and logical this time but actually right.

After a while, Randi took hold of my T-shirt sleeve and turned me toward the door.

"Come on, Carl," she said. "Whatever gross thing he said to hurt your feelings, just remember, it's only Dustin."

sixteen

The weather changed that night. The wind became cold, damp, and gusty. Sitting on the porch swing after dinner, I kept hearing oak leaves skitter across the floor like spiders.

"Why'd you tell me that sentence wrong?" I whispered, testing.

My stomach lurched. I wanted to throw up. I stopped the moving swing because it was making me dizzy.

The screen door screeched, and Daddy came out. He picked up Twink and put her in my lap, then sat down beside me.

"Thought I heard you talking to somebody out here," he said, stretching one arm behind my shoulders.

"Just Twink," I said. "Daddy, you know that flat brown stuff you and Noah take with you when you hunt sometimes? To eat for a snack? What's it called?"

"Jerky," he answered. "Beef jerky."

"Is it . . . good?"

"Oh, it's all right. It's not exactly supposed to taste good, but it keeps us going. Why?"

"Nothing," I said huskily. "I just wondered."

A dark shape flew over our barn—a monster with a single bright eye and slashing wings and talons.

"Another helicopter!" Mom exclaimed, coming out the screen door with a big afghan over her arm. "At night, yet," she added more softly.

"More state police 'copters going toward the river bottom," Daddy told her. He squeezed my knee and stood up. "Don't stay out here in the cold too long, C.B.," he said, then winked at me and went back into the house.

I felt the afghan being tucked around me, under my shoulders and legs and over Twink. It felt so wonderful, so warm and cozy that Twink immediately sank into a heavy ball on my legs. The tears that had been burning in my forehead leaked out the corners of my eyes, so I quickly brought the afghan over my nose to blot them.

"I know more about the Groats than you think," I snuffled up to Mom. "I know Dustin's mother drowned three falls ago and that Noah was going with Dustin's big sister when she got taken out of school."

I'd definitely taken her by surprise. The swing gyrated as she dropped down beside me. "Now, who's been talking to you about all that? Why can't people just quit gossiping in this town and let old wounds heal!"

"And everybody was relieved when Noah and Julie got separated, weren't they? Because Noah had to be protected. It's like . . . like the Groats are gross old . . . bugs or something."

"Oh, Carly," she said sadly. "I know it's hard to understand, but we were always more afraid that Julie's father or her uncles might do something to *her*, because they didn't want her . . . mixing. So, yes. I admit, in a way we were relieved, though Noah was miserable for a while. And now we always worry about Julie."

"Why do you worry about Julie?"

She reached over and pushed some damp hair off my cheek. "Carly, when her mother drowned, Julie was so lost. The town, the school, everyone was so worried about her and Dustin, but those men, those Groats, well, they wouldn't let us help. They never take advantage of the school's programs to help people, or the church's, or the town's. They're too suspicious to let anyone approach those awful walls they've built around themselves. Julie was fourteen, barely older than you, when her mother died, so maybe you can imagine how it would have been for her."

"It would be horrible," I whispered. "Especially if you were alone, without even friends."

"And Dustin. You kept coming home from school that awful fall and talking about how wild he was acting, and that broke my heart. He was so clearly crying out for attention. So many of us watched helplessly and worried."

I sat up straight and searched her eyes in the shadows. "Mom, don't be mad, but I heard you and the Arnetts talking and I can't get your conversation out of my mind. What do you mean when you say 'that awful fall'?"

She looked surprised, but not mad. She leaned back in the swing, sighing.

"Three summers ago, the Groats got mad at the town because we voted to open the new landfill out at the river bottom. They insisted that everything out there belonged to them, though actually most of the land out there is owned by the state, even some of the land that fence of theirs takes in. Anyway, to protest, they began shooting in Kosh Woods. Not hunting, which would have been bad enough, but just shooting, like they were living in the Wild West. It was pretty obvious they were doing drugs and drinking out there, too. It was nerve-wracking for everyone because you couldn't predict what they'd think of to do next. And I was terrified one of you kids would wander into the woods—I couldn't take my eyes off you for a second. Our local police were overwhelmed by the situation, but finally the state police cracked down."

"Cracked down?" I whispered. "How?"

"Several of the ringleaders, including Dustin's father, were jailed. For once, they spent time in the penitentiary, instead of just our local jail. Since then they've kept to themselves and stewed silently out there. Oh, they start a fight in some bar occasionally, or a few of them get in trouble for some sort of mischief around town. But things haven't come to a real flashpoint again."

She crossed her arms and looked toward the woods, and even in the darkness I could see a spark of fear in her eyes. She may as well have said what she was really thinking, that things hadn't come to a flashpoint again *yet*.

I licked my lips. "You and Mrs. Arnett said the word 'tragedy,' " I prodded. "What tragedy? Dustin's mother drowning?"

I could barely hear her answer: "If only the police had stopped things sooner. If only the town had found a way to help Melodie and the kids, to get them away until things calmed down. Melodie . . . left a note, just two words—'*No More.*' Julie found the note, but no one found Melodie until nearly a week after she drowned herself."

Though I could hardly breathe, I tried not to let on that Mom had just let slip one more word than I'd known before—*herself.* Dustin's mother had killed herself. So that was why no one had told us little third graders, Dustin's classmates. The death of a parent would have been carefully explained to us, but suicide was another thing, more like a crime or at least a guilty secret. Mom could barely speak of it even now.

We sat there quietly together, not even moving the swing. Mom reached for my hand.

"You can go in," I pushed out after a while. "I'll be in soon, okay?"

She stayed awhile longer and finally hugged me and silently went inside.

When she was gone, I took a deep breath. "Why'd you tell me that sentence wrong?" I whispered, testing.

My stomach lurched. I felt like throwing up.

And then I heard Dustin's beautiful, sad recorder music begin in Kosh Woods. Tonight there was a sort of drum beat behind it, mixing with it, ripping into it in a herky-jerky disorganized way that eventually penetrated the thick, soupy gloom in my brain.

I threw off the afghan and ran into the yard, hoping I wasn't hearing right. That sounded like the popcorn crack of rifle fire!

Was someone shooting in Kosh Woods?

seventeen

At first I thought I was just in a strange, confused mood when class started the next morning. But after about five minutes, anyone with the slightest bit of radar could have told that doom was about to fall. Ms. Aspen not only looked pinched up around the face, but she spoke in this sharp, steely way.

"I. Am. So. Disappointed." She sounded like we'd shot her full of holes and wind was whistling through her.

Leigh Ann jumped to her feet. "Ms. Aspen, I didn't have anything to do with it! I swear on a stack of Bibles!"

"Please take. Your seat," Ms. Aspen wheezed, pinching that little piece of nose that goes between your eyes.

The only part of her long lecture I listened closely to

111

was how she'd found out about the interview switches. Cassie had evidently come to her after class yesterday, whining about how it wasn't fair for her to have to interview Todd now when she hated his guts and everybody else was interviewing their best friends or boyfriends.

Cassie has never been what you would call brilliant. While people turned to glare at her, Ms. Aspen got to our punishment. A couple of canceled recesses, extra homework, no gum on gum day, and if anything like this happened again, no field trip to Worlds of Fun in May.

"The interview assignment is canceled, of course. I'm not even sure at this point that you have the maturity to handle having a class newspaper. I'll decide that later. We obviously can't choose an editor by audition, so if I do decide to let you have a paper, we'll just take a vote to see who gets the job."

Randi and Alicia both gasped and looked at me like they were afraid I was about to go ballistic.

And I guess about nine days before, the day we'd first gotten the assignment, I would have. After all, a vote is usually a popularity contest, not a real test of your ability, like an audition.

But though I'd tried and tried to think of him as *only* Dustin, like Randi had told me I should, there hadn't been a single minute in the last twenty-four hours when I hadn't wondered how I was going to face Dustin again, now that he'd asked me that awful question.

So to tell the truth, the main reaction I had to Ms. Aspen's announcement was relief.

Still, I couldn't get through my head that Dustin wasn't my project any longer. I kept glancing over my shoulder at him. Every time I looked, he was slouched in his usual position, his recorder balanced carefully in his pencil slot, his frog like a faint, uneven heart-beat.

His left arm seemed worse today. He'd held it against his side in a funny way all week, but when we were dismissed for music class that morning, I noticed it hung loglike as he ambled down the hall.

And during music class, he held his recorder in his right hand but didn't even attempt to get it out of its felt cocoon. When we paused for a two-measure rest in the middle of "Old MacDonald," Eric waved his hand wildly in the air. "Mr. Norville! Mr. Norville! Dustin isn't playing."

Everybody looked at Dustin, but Dustin just kept staring expressionlessly at his own knees.

Mr. Norville was peeved, but mostly with Eric, not Dustin. "Mr. Gilman, when the conductor's baton is in the air, what don't we do?"

"Interrupt the music," Eric and a few other people chanted.

"Thank you." Mr. Norville raised his baton again, and we went squawking on like a bunch of chickens.

*   *   *

113

"Pee-euuw! We really, really stunk today," Alicia said as we waited in the cafeteria line after music.

"We were rotten," Jasmine agreed, nodding so enthusiastically she almost seemed proud of that fact.

"I couldn't figure out what we were playing enough to even play," Randi complained. "What was wrong with you guys, anyhow?"

"Can't you figure it out?" I asked them. "Who wasn't playing today that usually makes us sound good?"

Everybody looked totally stumped.

"Well, me?" Randi finally guessed, looking around to see what was happening in the cafeteria. Her eyes came to a stop and she put her hands on her hips. "Just *look* at that! Sixth-grade boys are *so* immature!"

We looked where she was looking. Josh Simon and Tim Garreuth were using their recorders to sword fight across the water fountain, while half of the other boys in our class were trying to crowd in close enough to get drenched.

Luke ran ahead when we got off the bus that afternoon. Noah and I trudged silently up the hill together, and when we got close to the house we could see that Daddy was in from the fields, sitting on the porch swing with his arm draped over Luke's shoulders. He pushed his baseball hat back so the tan line across his forehead showed.

"Before you two disappear, let's make us some

lemonade," Daddy called out, which meant he wanted to talk to us about something.

Inside the house, he got right to the point.

"I need your word on something, kids," he said as he began cutting the lemons in half with his pocketknife. "I need you to promise me you won't go into Kosh-kanong Woods this weekend. Or anytime, until I say it's okay."

Noah took down four huge plastic cups and began dumping half a tray of ice cubes into each of them.

Daddy waited till the noise of that was over, then explained, "When I was cutting hay over near the woods this afternoon, I heard gunfire back there. Kosh Woods has been a game reserve, out-of-bounds for hunting since long before I was a boy. But there've been times over the years when the sheriff has had a little trouble enforcing that, and this fall is looking like one of those times."

Then I *had* heard gunfire back there the night before. The Groats?

"But it's a free country!" Luke piped from where he was standing on Mom's stepstool, ready to add the sugar.

I rolled my eyes, and Daddy quit squeezing the lemons and leaned forward on his elbows to get down to Luke's eye level.

"Son, think about that a little. Everyone around here wants to have freedom to walk in the woods, to collect nuts, to fish in the creek. But some people want to have freedom to shoot guns and hunt out there. Now, don't you see how dangerous it would be to combine those two freedoms? Everybody can't always have everything they want. That's why we have laws and why we vote about which freedoms we're willing to put aside to keep others. That's just how it has to work."

Luke's round face registered confusion. "But George Washington said . . ."

"George Washington didn't live in the same neck of the woods as those Groats!" Noah said angrily, bringing the ice cube tray down hard on the counter.

All three of us looked at him. Noah gets angry so seldom you can hardly believe it when you see it.

"Are you through, Dad?" Noah asked. His face looked white, and his neck blotchy red. "I gotta do my homework."

"Go," Daddy said. "As long as everybody understands. There's to be a town meeting Monday night, so maybe we can get things straightened out then. But in the meantime, Carly?"

"Right. No going into the woods." I concentrated on chasing the seeds out of the lemon juice, then turned on the cold water to add to the pitcher. I was so worried about Noah, and something, an idea, maybe a really bad one, was wiggling into my brain in spite of my trying to keep it out.

I slid the pitcher over to Luke, whose job it is to

dump about a ton of sugar all over the counter, eventually getting some into the lemonade. When he was done, I stirred, Daddy filled our glasses, and we drank standing up in the kitchen, all of us looking at Noah's empty glass.

I had to do it. I just had to, bad idea or not.

"Lucas Henry, let's go sharpen the blades on the mower," Daddy said, putting his empty cup in the sink and tugging lightly on Lukey's sleeve.

I knew that out in the barn, Daddy would keep talking about this dangers-of-freedom idea until he was convinced it had finally sunk deep enough into Luke's innocent brain.

Meanwhile, I had to talk to another person with a dangerous brain at the moment—Noah.

I knocked on his door, then opened it. He was lying on the floor with his feet up on his bed and some books spread out on his stomach, slamming a tennis ball against the wall then catching it. His radio was going full blast, and I walked over and turned it off.

"Hey." He looked in my direction.

"Okay, Noah, here's the deal," I said, sitting on the edge of his bed. "I'm only telling you this because you're so zonked out right now that I'm worried you'll go back to the Groat compound and get your stupid head shot off."

"What are you talking about, Carl?" Noah asked, and

something in his eyes told me that yes, he *would* keep driving around that compound. He wasn't even bothering to deny it or tell me I was crazy.

I took a deep breath. "Maybe there's a safe place you and Julie could meet. See, there's this tunnel that connects the compound to Kosh Woods. And, uh, I happen to know exactly where the entrance is."

Half an hour later I had a note from Noah to Julie tucked deep inside my book bag, asking her to meet him in the tunnel. I'd promised to give it to Dustin Monday morning and to ask him to deliver it to his sister.

Though I'd hoped never to have to talk to Dustin again, I kept telling myself this would be over in just one minute, maybe less. Forty-five or even thirty seconds.

I could surely keep my mind a blank and stand anything for a mere few seconds.

eighteen

Early the next morning there were loud, excited voices in our kitchen. As I stumbled out into the hall, I nearly broke my neck over Noah, who was sitting cross-legged in the shadows at the top of the stairs, listening.

"What's going on?" I mouthed.

"Some of the chief gossips in town are talking to Dad about the Groats," he whispered.

"About the shooting in the woods?" I asked as I plopped down beside him.

Noah held up a hand to tell me to be quiet and listen.

I figured out who was down there from their voices, and also from that "chief gossip" hint Noah had given. Mr. Arnett; Mr. Renfrow, who, besides farming, worked part-time at the service station; and Mrs. Jackson, the postmistress.

". . . of course, for years we've put up with them

stringing their beer cans around the countryside like—like Christmas-tree lights!" Mrs. Jackson was saying. "But lately that appears to be the least of our worries!"

"Weeeell, you know," Mr. Renfrow drawled, and I could picture him leaning back on his heels, putting his hands deep in his overall pockets, settling in to make a big long speech, "it's bad they got them a methamphetamine lab going, I'm not about to say it's not. The marijuana growing's been bad, and this is worse. Why, every other week or so you read in the papers about some fool around these hills having a meth lab, having it blow up in his face. I mean, methamphetamine is a cheap and easy drug to make. Lord, they use such things as drain cleaner and gasoline to do it! But now, this new thing." He made the little sound my dad uses, too, when something's really bad. "Uhm, um, um."

This new thing? I frowned at Noah, and again he shrugged.

"All day yesterday people kept coming to the post office and talking about how the Groats were running all around Koshkanong Woods, dressed in camouflage outfits from the Army surplus store in Kansas City," Mrs. Jackson said in her quick, fluttery way. "Running around the woods in broad daylight, they were! Shooting and playing at their war games! In our woods! Where there could be children!"

"Well, Sol Groat's been talking over at Smitty's Bar, sayin' they gotta train for military action 'cause the government's about to start a second civil war," Mr. Arnett said.

I was dying to call down and ask him if Mrs. Arnett knew he was spending time in Smitty's Bar.

"Them new friends of theirs," he continued, "these fellas they've been meeting up with at gun shows, has told them the government could attack at any time, and they're ready to believe such nonsense. They're claiming those helicopters hovering over their compound this past week proves it! Now looks like they're stockpiling guns, and bragging openly of it."

"Well, the town can surely put a stop to all this at the town meeting Monday night!" Mrs. Jackson interjected, sounding like she'd been waiting forever for her chance to talk. "But meanwhile, Mr. Cameron, we came over to beg you to do anything you can to get through to them."

"Ron, you're the only one they'll listen to," Mr. Arnett agreed. "They still consider you a friend."

Finally, Daddy got a word in edgewise. Actually, two. "Too late," he said. Then in a softer, sadder voice, he added, "I'll try, but I expect it's just too late."

When they finally left, I decided to go back to bed. It was a blustery, damp, and chilly day, and I fell into a cozy sleep.

When I woke up again I pulled on jeans and a sweatshirt and went downstairs, but I couldn't find anybody. Mom was working at the library, I knew, and Daddy was probably out in the machinery shed. I supposed Noah was in the machine shed, too, working on that hopeless old car.

But where was Luke? Then I suddenly heard him.

"Hold *still* now, you silly cat! Twink, I *mean* it!"

I hustled across the kitchen and out the screen door, and found Luke kneeling on the gray boards of the front porch floor, trying to tape Twinkletoes to a big piece of cardboard.

Personally, I thought Twinkletoes was doing an amazing job of holding still, considering the circumstances. She was on her back with her feet curled in the air, and only her tail was moving, swishing furiously back and forth. Her eyes were wide, and she was growling deep in her throat.

I crouched quickly beside them. "Luke, you can't tape Twinkletoes! It'll pull out her fur! How would *you* like it if somebody tried to tape *you?* And anyway, what are you . . . doing?"

Luke sighed loudly and sat back on his heels. Twink saw her chance, did a sleek little twisting flip to her feet, and slid shadowlike from the porch and into the bushes.

"Carly! Now I'll never catch her!"

Luke was sweaty in spite of the cold drizzle the wind was driving across the porch. There was a huge ball of discarded masking tape and cat fur beside him. I could tell he'd been struggling with this hopeless project for a long, long time.

"Luke, what in the world were you trying to do?"

His chin began to quiver. "We have to draw something for art, and I can't draw. I thought if I taped Twinkletoes down I could draw around her like we drew around our hands in kindergarten."

It took me a few seconds to decide how to go on with this conversation. "Sure you can draw, Luke," I finally said.

"No," he said firmly. "I drew a horse, and Bryce said it was a Tyrannosaurus Rex."

"Well, those look quite a bit alike."

"I drew a spaceship, and Bryce called it a pencil."

Noah appeared and took the six porch stairs in two strides, wiping grease from his hands onto a rag. He was looking more like the old, cheerful Noah again, now that he had a plan for meeting Julie.

"Sounds to me like Bryce just doesn't know beans about art," Noah told Luke.

"Right!" I agreed. "Artists are always having to put up with people thinking they can't draw, or dance, or whatever it is they're doing. Listen, Luke, we'll expand my hayloft poetry studio into an art and poetry studio, okay? You can work on your art this afternoon and tomorrow while I practice poetry and recorder."

"Really?" Luke piped, bouncing excitedly on his knees.

"I'll help you move your art supplies into the hayloft as soon as I get cleaned up," Noah offered. "Just remember—no going up there without me or Carly, okay?"

Noah and I didn't exactly know what we were getting ourselves into. Ever since he learned to toddle, Luke has collected things he picks up off the ground—acorns, Dairy Queen straws, pop-can tabs, feathers, you name it. He has a separate paper grocery sack for each thing, and he wanted every single one of those sacks taken up into the hayloft.

We made quick sandwiches for lunch, then Noah began dragging Luke's stuff up the hayloft ladder while I helped Luke organize it once it got there.

"There, your majesty," I said when I finally plunked the last two sacks down on the hayloft floor. "Are you sure there isn't anything else? The refrigerator, maybe, or your bed, perhaps?"

"The whole family uses the refrigerator, Carly," Luke said stiffly. "And I'm not supposed to sleep up here, remember?"

Because it took most of Saturday to get Luke settled in, it was Sunday afternoon before he and I spent time in our shared studio actually working.

I sat with my legs dangling out the hayloading window, looking across the fields, with my poetry notebook open to a fresh page. The air was clear and cool and clean, after yesterday's drizzle. The only sounds were the locusts and a combine or two.

Behind me, Luke kept rummaging in his sacks, making this important, busy noise, almost like he was

Michelangelo or Picasso or someone. The breeze flipped through the pages of my notebook, and when I looked back down, *Earbug* was staring up at me.

I snapped shut my notebook and tossed it aside, then crawled through the mounds of clutter on Luke's side of the studio to check out what he was working on.

"It's that newspaper hat Daddy made you! What are you . . . doing to it?"

"Fixing it up by gluing stuff to it," Luke answered in this voice that told me he was concentrating and didn't want to be disturbed.

I went back over near the window and picked up my recorder, hoping I'd gotten better since last time I'd played.

"Shhh, listen, Carly!" Luke suddenly exclaimed in a whisper. "It's the Goatboy mugician!"

Sure enough, Dustin was playing now, out in Kosh Woods.

I got as close as I could to the edge of the window, stretched my arms like wings to grab tight to both rough oak sides, and leaned out, listening. His music had gone in these few days from being pretty and simple to being beautiful and complicated. But still, what you heard most clearly was the sadness weaving through it.

"Uh, Luke?" I was surprised to feel my heart beating a little faster. "Did I tell you that the magical Goatboy was . . . a rotten student? Well, I mean, way back in first grade, then in second, he did okay on his work.

But in third grade, when he was doing all that cussing and spitting and kicking and stuff? Well, he didn't pay attention to his schoolwork one tiny bit. He was always lost because he never followed along with the lesson."

I pulled in from the window, crossed my arms, and leaned back against the rough oak sill. I closed my eyes. I could feel sunshine on the right half of my face, and dark, damp shadows on the left half.

When Luke didn't say anything, I glanced at him. He was squatting over his project, working away, but listening, too, I could tell.

"But Caralotta, the good fairy, well, she was a wonderful student, just like you are now."

"Bryce says I'm almost one of the best," Luke mentioned.

I nodded. "You do your homework and study hard, just like Caralotta did. So well, see, one day the teacher suddenly called on the Goatboy to read a sentence in the reading book aloud. But the Goatboy hadn't been paying attention at all, and so . . . so he leaned over and asked Caralotta for help, and Caralotta . . ."

Why had I started this? You should never tell fairy tales when you're in a bad mood. They don't come out magic, they just come out . . . real. And depressing.

"Caralotta what, Carly?" Luke asked. "Caralotta what!"

I licked my lips and rushed to finish. "Caralotta told him the wrong sentence to read, because she thought it would be a good lesson for him about the importance of paying attention and stuff. She did that because she was nice, always thinking about other people."

"She was mean to the Goatboy!" Luke insisted. "I *told* you she was mean! She was one of those mean people that made him take his wooden whistle like Grandpa made me and go live in a lonely corner of the woods and be invisible!"

"She was not! You should listen more closely, Luke." Suddenly I could hardly breathe, and I just wanted to throw something. "Come on, we're going down. I'm sick of it up here."

nineteen

Because I was still upset on the bus the next morning, and also nervous about having to give Dustin that note, I snapped at Randi.

"What's that on your brother's head?" she asked.

I shrugged. "He made it. At first Mom wouldn't let him wear it to school, but he finally wore her down."

"Weird." She giggled.

"For your information, it happens to be art. Everything isn't weird or dumb or 'only' just because you say it is, Randi."

She just gaped at me, and Alicia quickly changed the subject to the science test we had coming up, which was a relief.

I spent a lot of time in class that morning glancing over my shoulder at Dustin, trying to get up my nerve.

Now that I actually had to do it, I couldn't picture myself just walking over and facing him, even for a few seconds.

On our way to lunch, Dustin, as usual, was bringing up the rear, lagging a few steps behind everybody else. I slouched against the wall, waiting for him to pull up even with me, then I whipped out the note and quickly thrust it at him.

"Here, give this to your sister," I said in a rush. "I mean, please. It's from my brother, I, uh, mean."

He crammed Noah's note into his pocket and looked down the hall. "She wants your brother to meet her tonight. She told me you should tell him that."

I nodded, swallowing. "Where?" I whispered.

"Under Chandler's Oak." He turned and looked right into my face. "In case you're worried, won't be no shooting out there tonight," he said. "They'll all be at the meeting in town. That's how she can get away, just this one time."

Jasmine grabbed my elbow then, though I hadn't even heard her running back down the hall. "What are you *doing*, Carl? Come *on!* Everybody's waiting for you!"

"Thanks, and tell her I'll tell him," I said in a rush to Dustin, then let myself be pulled toward my friends, who were standing in a bright cluster, waiting for me.

"Was Dustin bothering you?" Krista whispered.

"Bothering me?" I wrinkled my nose. "No! Why'd you think that? We were just talking."

She looked at Jasmine and they both shrugged.

"Whatever," Randi said, "as long as you're sure you're okay."

We'd reached the big arched entrance to the cafeteria, and I looked back over my shoulder before we went in. There was glaring sunshine coming in the open doorway at the far end of the hall. Dustin was still standing alone, circled by the light behind him so the glare erased all his details. He could have been a paper doll being burned up from all its edges.

Or a Goatboy in the process of becoming invisible.

The events of the next hour turned out to be so important that I've gone over them a million times in my mind.

After we finished eating, I went with Alicia and Randi to the gym. They started jazz dancing, and I sat with my back against the tiles of the gym wall and opened my poetry notebook.

I remember I tried to work on my poetry, but I couldn't get into it. I looked over toward the bleachers a few times. It was getting chilly outside, so Ms. Trinny was letting the kindergarteners stay in the gym for noon recess. They sat playing a circle game near the bottom bleacher.

I remember narrowing my eyes and peering into the deep triangle of shadows between the bleachers and the door of the gym. I imagined Dustin under the bleachers, skulking around in the cobwebs below the gum-covered underneaths of the seats, hiding there in the gloom mere inches behind the unsuspecting kindergarteners. He'd make a dash for the door, through that shadowy triangle, after the bell rang and everyone else was gone.

And then suddenly, so suddenly I doubted my own eyes, Dustin appeared in the triangle of shadow. He was crouching, animal-like, facing the open expanse of hardwood floor where Alicia and Randi spun and ran and whirled to the beat.

I was shocked that he'd show himself like that, come out of his forbidden territory while noon recess was still going on. There were tons of ways he could get into big-time trouble, I remember thinking. If Randi saw him, she'd accuse him of spying. If a teacher saw him, she'd think he'd been doing something awful and secret there in the darkness. If one of the kindergarteners pointed at him, their teacher would jump on him, too. Ms. Trinny was always worrying about somebody sneaking up and hurting or at least scaring a kindergartener.

I glanced nervously around the gym, as though I were Dustin's lookout. I almost think I noticed for one microsecond how cheerful and alive the gym looked. It was like watching a beautiful video about Africa. The basketball boys seemed like giraffes, the dancers like gazelles, the kindergarteners like colorful little parrots.

But then a cloud must have gone over the sun, because almost instantly the gym got dark and clammy, like when the video camera catches the cougar skulking behind the bush and your stomach sinks because you instantly know this is going to be one of those "food chain" videos where something eats something else.

"Watch this, Carly!" Randi called, and I automatically jerked my eyes toward where she was doing a bouncy sidestep thing that ended in a high kick. Alicia was behind her and off to the left, her arms out at her sides. Her chin was high, her face dreamy, and she was balancing on her toes, moving in a fast glide across the polished floor.

I saw all this in a quick glance, then I looked back to the triangle of shadow by the bleachers.

Dustin was running out into the open gym, right toward Randi and Ali!

". . . five, six, seven, *eight!*" Randi sang out.

In the distance, Mr. Hendershot barked some kind of order to the basketball players, and I realized I'd been straining forever to make the irregular rubber thump of the ball synchronize with the loud, pulsing beat of the music on Randi's tape.

Then, right then, all the warring gym noises suddenly dimmed into the background and I heard the silence of something becoming airborne. Then came the sickening thud of something hitting the hardwood gym floor, some soft, loosely-held-together thing that sounded totally unprepared for the smack of gravity.

My stomach churned, and I put my head down on my knees, holding my breath.

"She falled!" I heard a little kindergartener squeal. "Yes, she *did* fall. See her? Right there!"

I jerked my head up just in time to see Dustin running away from Randi and Ali and on out of the gym. I jumped up and ran, too, then, to crouch beside Alicia, where she sprawled on the floor maybe twenty yards from where I'd been sitting. Her cinnamon eyes were wide in her pale face, and she stared at her arm, which had a big U-shaped hump a little above the wrist.

"That's not mine," she whispered, her chin quivering.

"She doesn't know what she's saying." Randi had reached Alicia's other side and crouched there, looking as pale as Alicia herself. Then she looked around us in panic. "Call Nurse Jasper!" she screamed to no one in particular, to everyone.

Mr. Hendershot and the basketball boys came thundering up. "Call Nurse Jasper!" Mr. Hendershot ordered, as though Randi hadn't just done that.

The basketball boys shuffled around in confusion.

"Now! On the double!" Mr. Hendershot barked, and a couple of them started running toward the double doors as Mr. Hendershot crouched with us and tore off his jacket to put over Alicia's shoulders.

The basketball boys nearly slammed into Nurse Jasper as she rushed in through the double doors, along with Ms. Trinny, who was frantic and pretending to be calm by talking too slowly. "Now . . . everything . . . is . . . just fine . . . A-okay . . . okay? . . . Okay!" she chanted in this too-slow, squeaky voice that scared you to death.

The kindergarteners were either whimpering softly or straining to get a better look as their teacher quickly corraled them and led them away.

"Doesn't seem like your arm should be able to *do* that," one of the basketball boys muttered, causing Mr. Hendershot to give him a red-eyed glare.

"Showers!" Mr. Hendershot barked. "Into the showers, team!" All the boys slunk sheepishly away, looking grossed out.

"That can't be it," Alicia said softly, shivering. Big tears tracked down her cheeks and matted some of her electric hair to the pillow Nurse Jasper had slipped under her head.

"Shhh, now, you'll be fine, Alicia." Nurse Jasper worked quickly and gently, loosely bracing Ali's arm against her body in a splint of aluminum and gauze. "Are you dizzy? No? Good. The ambulance is on its way, so just breathe deep and relax for me."

"Nurse Jasper?" Randi was staring at Alicia's leg. Alicia had landed facedown, but Mr. Hendershot and Nurse Jasper had carefully turned her over, so her arm could be braced. "Look . . ." Randi swallowed. "Uh, look at this."

We all looked, Randi and Nurse Jasper and Ms. Trinny and Mr. Hendershot and I. Alicia's left knee was all puffy and red, and something awful was oozing out of it.

Something slimy, yellowish-brown, and red.

twenty

We may as well not have had school that afternoon. All of us, Ms. Aspen included, were way too jittery to get anything done. Nurse Jasper went with Alicia in the ambulance. She said she'd call the school the second she knew anything, and Ms. Trinny promised she'd come and tell the sixth grade first, but by the end of the afternoon, we were still waiting.

Dustin Groat didn't come back to class after lunch. No one seemed surprised, or even mentioned it.

The bus drivers always slouched against the bike racks as we got on the buses in the afternoon, and I heard two of them talking as we boarded.

"Them Groats," one of them said, and spat tobacco on the ground, "they ought to be hanged at birth, the whole pack of 'em."

"Menace to society," the other driver agreed.

From that, I was pretty positive that everybody in Cooper's Glade already knew about Alicia's accident and blamed Dustin for it.

Noah sat right behind Randi and me on the bus going home, and Randi kept talking over her shoulder to him in this breathless, dramatic voice. "Every single person in the gym saw him trip her. I mean, there must have been at least twenty witnesses, not even counting the kindergarteners."

I'd been looking out the window, trying to see through the grime the weekend's drizzle had left on the glass. I turned to her. "Why do you keep telling everyone he tripped her, Randi?"

She frowned at me. "Everybody saw it, Carl! You surely saw it yourself, didn't you?"

"I saw Dustin run in front of her, and I saw her trip over him and fall," I said. "Someone tripping over you isn't the same as you tripping them. And the way you say 'witnesses,' you make it sound like Dustin's going to stand trial or something."

Randi pulled her foot up under her so her knee was on the seat, as if she wanted to cover up the awful space that Alicia had left. "Carly, think about it. He was probably hiding under the bleachers. He was even camouflaged to match the bleachers and the floor, like he'd planned it down to the last detail!"

"He always wears brown," I said. "Mud brown."

I couldn't think of a way to tell her he'd been hiding under the bleachers for over a week now. How would I explain not telling her (warning her, she'd say) when I'd first found out?

Randi shivered and dropped her voice to a whisper. "Well, you wouldn't be defending him, Carly, if *you'd* been his target."

And then, just as I was getting really ticked with her, Randi's eyes teared up, and seeing that made my own throat ache.

"I'm so scared, Carl." Randi bit her lip. "That awful stuff coming out of her knee . . ."

I could only nod, linking my pinky finger through Randi's, a thing we'd done a lot when we were little.

Randi squeezed my pinky with hers.

In the seat behind us, Noah just cracked his knuckles and didn't say a word.

When we got off the bus, Lukey scurried on up the hill, and Noah and I just stood watching him, listlessly staring at his amazing hat.

"So." Noah sank cross-legged into the deep patch of wild sunflowers beside the road. "You don't think Dustin did it? Or what?"

"Oh, Alicia tripped over him, all right. He ran right in front of her." I sat beside him, snatched a dandelion head to depetal, and sighed.

"But . . . ?" Noah asked.

"But, well . . . why? Why would he do something like that? Noah, Dustin doesn't try to get attention. Well, he did when he was a little kid, like Luke. We were all pretty flaky then. But now he . . . hides. He hates attention. Everybody is going crazy with worry over Alicia, but what about Dustin's arm? It's been hurting lately. Maybe at home they hit him. You saw him run out of the house that day. You saw how scared and angry he was."

I threw my handful of loose petals into the air. "It just bothers me that if anybody else in class had hurt someone, people would ask why. With Dustin, the 'why' is because he's 'one of those Groats.'"

Noah didn't say anything. His face was all angles, with a curl of shiny dark hair looping over his left eye. When he was thinking hard like this, his eyes turned to deep-blue pools.

"By the way," I told him, pretending I didn't know it was what he was dying to hear about, "I gave Dustin your note, but he said Julie wants you to meet her at Chandler's Oak tonight. He said the Groats will all be at the town meeting, so there won't be any shooting."

Noah gulped, then gave a slight nod.

"Go on in, Noah. Don't worry about me. I'm mostly just really worried about Alicia, so I'm going up to the hayloft for a while. Tell Mom that's where I am, okay?"

"Right," he said, reaching over to yank my hair. "Thanks, Carl, for . . . you know."

Just then, Mom came out onto the porch, cupped her hands around her mouth, and called down the hill to me.

"Car-lee! Hurry inside! Alicia's on the phone!"

"She's home!" I unwound the kitchen phone cord from my arm. It left teensy tractor-tire marks from my wrist to my elbow, and my hand felt tingly as I hung up the receiver. "Alicia's already home from the hospital! She broke both bones right above her wrist, and her knee's bruised, but she doesn't have to have an operation or anything like that. She's okay!"

Mom replaced the lid on the chili she'd been stirring. "Oh, thank goodness," she said, putting her hands, one on top of the other, on her chest.

Alicia had said on the phone that the gunk on her knee hadn't been leaking out from inside her after all. "It was foreign matter," she'd said in the precise way some doctor must have said it to her. "From some external source."

"And she said since no skin or muscle was torn, she can come back to school in a day or two," I told Mom. "And after her cast comes off, she can go right back to doing gymnastics again."

I slid to the floor with my back pressed against the wall and hugged my knees. Luke came into the kitchen, and I grabbed him and pulled him onto my lap. "She's okay, she's okay, she's okay!" I trapped him with my knees and tickled him and kissed his sweaty neck over and over again until he started poking me in the ribs with his sharp elbows.

"You're gonna mess up my hat, Carly!" he yelled.

"Luke, into the bathroom to wash those hands," Mom ordered. "Carly, time to set the table."

I released Luke and he raced away. I still felt slaphappy, and I danced around the kitchen as I got down the plates.

"Claire and Sam must be so relieved," Mom whispered, wiping her eyes quickly on her apron.

"Uh, Mom? Where am I supposed to put the glasses?"

Luke had constructed a centerpiece for the kitchen table, a blob of clay and hamburger wrappers with turkey feathers sticking out of it in all directions.

"Work around it," Mom said softly, without even having to ask what I was talking about.

twenty-one

I really wanted to go to the town meeting that night, but I didn't get to.

"It's sort of an adult thing, Carly," Daddy mumbled when I went outside after dinner to ask about going. He was taking feed sacks out of the truck, and I tagged at his heels, kicking the dirt.

Mom came onto the porch, fanning her face with the dish towel, and I ran over to work on her instead.

"Hey, Mom, I think I should get to go to the meeting tonight. Otherwise, how am I going to learn about current events and stuff? And I bet Randi gets to go." I'd started to say I bet Noah got to, but I'd caught myself just in time. Noah's plans for the night didn't need to be made public, that was for sure.

"Honey, I think every voter in Cooper's Glade should be at the meeting tonight, which means your dad and me both," she told me. "I really don't think Randi or any other young people will be there. And, frankly, I was sort of hoping you could take Luke aside while we're gone and maybe, well, talk to him. He listens to you, probably more than to anyone."

"Talk to him about what?" I whispered, flattered.

"About his, well . . . about his silly . . ."

I thought I knew what she was getting at. His silly, annoying ideas about honesty and freedom. Luke definitely spent too much time lately noticing how the rest of us fell short of being perfect, George Washington–type people.

". . . his silly hat," she finished, shaking her head. "He won't take it off, even to take a bath. But he just can't keep wearing that awful thing to school!"

I guess she hadn't noticed that this afternoon he'd also made himself a pop-can-tab belt. It was obvious to me that the hat was only the beginning, a sort of root system a whole outfit was starting to grow from, but I didn't want to worry her more by mentioning that.

When Mom and Daddy took off for the meeting, I found Luke on the sloping tin roof of one of the pig houses. I'd been right—the hat had been only the beginning. He had a pile of old corncobs beside him, and he was painstakingly shoving the smallest of them through the pop-can tabs his belt was made of.

"Uh, Luke? Hi. Whatcha up to?"

He had his toy binoculars with him, swinging from

142

their plastic cord around his neck. He raised them to his eyes and swiveled toward me. "Who goes there?"

"Your sister."

"Permission granted to come aboard."

"Aye, aye, Captain."

I carefully pushed down the barbed wire and climbed over the short pig-pen fence, then hoisted myself up onto the pig-house roof.

"You know, Luke, I've been doing some thinking about your great hat," I said, as I'd planned. "I'm not so sure you should wear it to school tomorrow. You should probably store it somewhere and keep it nice, just in case."

He looked at me. "In case what?"

I shrugged, feeling, I admit, pretty clever. "Oh, you know, in case George Washington shows up to visit your class or something. If he did, you'd want something really artistic to wear, right? So if I were you . . ."

"George Washington's dead, Carly," Luke interrupted. "Didn't you know that? And I want to tell you something important."

He leaned close to me and whispered, "I just discovered the castle of Lucas the Magnificent." He raised his binoculars to his eyes again, aiming them across the soybean field, toward Kosh Woods. He jerked up his skinny arm and pointed. "There!" he exclaimed. "It's the castle tower, sticking up higher than anything in the world. From up in his castle tower, Lucas the Magnificent can see everything that's going on in the kingdom."

Luke was pointing at the jagged, orange-leafed top of Chandler's Oak. I'd never noticed before that from here at the very edge of our barnyard you could see it sprangling wider-branched and a little above all the other trees in Kosh Woods.

I sighed. An hour from now, when it was completely dark and the town meeting was well underway and there was time for Julie to sneak away through the night, she and Noah would be standing right under that tree, with only the purple-faced moon watching them. I pictured Noah holding up his hand and Julie putting hers against it, palm to palm.

Would they, like . . . kiss?

When Mom and Daddy finally got home, it was late and I was in bed. But I could hear them sitting in the kitchen talking, so I sneaked over and sat at the top of the stairway.

". . . never seen so many guns in my life," Mom was saying, her voice sharp, like she talked to us when we were doing something she knew we knew better than to do. "There must have been twenty in the back of that truck of theirs, and they had the gall to park where you had to walk right by them."

"They just brought those guns along to flaunt 'em," Daddy said. He lowered his voice and laughed in this strange way. "I doubt it makes you feel better, but I'm sure they had three or four hidden away in that compound for every one they brought along to show off. You heard 'em—they're preparing for civil war. They expect those black helicopters that have been sniffing around out there to start it any minute, and they want to be ready to hold on to what's theirs."

"What they *consider* to be theirs, like Koshkanong Woods," Mom said in that same sharp way. "It doesn't occur to them those helicopters want to take away their illegal drugs, not what they kept calling their 'Second Amendment right to bear arms.' I just wanted to slap Sarge Groat's face when he stood up and yelled all that about how they're taking back the woods and how the time for corrupt government laws trying to stop them is over."

"You woulda had to hurry, seeing as how they all stormed out right after that. I don't know which was more aggravating—having them shout down anybody who took the floor to speak, or having them walk out like that after they said their piece."

They both were quiet then for a while. Finally, I heard a sound that I think was Mom crying, really softly. Sniffling.

"Hey, hey, now," Daddy said.

"Well, I can't help it, Ron," she said quietly. "I'm scared. You felt it just like I did. Sure we voted to put tighter restrictions on the woods, but if they're determined to have their way, there won't be any real way of keeping them from having it. I wouldn't be a bit surprised if they weren't back out in the woods right now, practicing those awful war games of theirs with a vengeance, just to be sure we all got the message."

I heard a rustling, swishy sound coming from behind my back. It was Noah, climbing the vines outside his bedroom window. I felt myself trembling all over, and I realized how scared I'd been, listening to them down in the kitchen, wondering if Noah was in danger after all. I crawled back from the landing and tiptoed in a crouch to his room.

"Noah?" I whispered, rapping lightly on his door.

Seconds later, he opened it a crack. "I saw her, Carl," he whispered back. "It was great. We talked. It was . . . great."

He must have thought I was curious about the juicy details of his meeting with Julie, but I slipped on through his door and hugged him, hard.

"I'm so glad you're home safe!" I told him, then, while he stood gawking in surprise, I turned and hurried back to my own room.

In bed, I covered my head with my pillow, but still, just like Mom had predicted, I heard heavy gunfire start up in Kosh Woods later that night. It sounded too fast and furious to be aimed at anything much but everybody's ears, which meant the Groats were still having their say, forcing everyone to listen.

twenty-two

Daddy came in from the fields at seven the next morning and sat all of us down for a serious talk, which was pretty much what I'd expected after what I'd overheard the night before.

As he warned us about the Groats' new activities and ordered us, again, to stay completely away from Kosh Woods, I let my mind wander. I was glad Mom was at work this morning because she would have flipped out over Luke's outfit—the hat, of course, and the corncob-stuffed pop-can-tab belt, and now he also had a snakeskin tied around his right leg, just above the knee.

". . . and since they wear those camouflage outfits now, they'll disappear into the trees and brush and they'll be more dangerous than ever," Daddy said, winding up his talk and standing to go outside. "It's a law that when you hunt you have to wear some hunter orange to show people you're around. But, of course, that probably won't make a rat's tail of difference to them."

"I'll bet they'll be shooting each other more than anything else, dressed so they're invisible like that," Noah said.

"Probably," Daddy agreed, sadly shaking his head.

"They become invisible?" Luke asked.

I could tell he was thinking about the Goatboy.

"They sort of disappear when they wear these camouflage clothes they've got," I explained. "It's hard to see them. Haven't you studied camouflage in science? Like, lions against the tall, brown grass? Butterflies with spots on their wings that look like the eyes of a predator? The Groats have outfits now that make them look like things in the woods, trees and stuff."

"Speaking of disappear, young man, you skitter upstairs and change into school clothes before you miss the bus," Daddy interrupted in his don't-even-think-about-arguing voice.

Mom must have given Daddy clothes orders before she left.

On the bus, Randi and I mostly talked about how relieved we were that Alicia was all right and coming back to school tomorrow, even though, Randi said, it was a shame that now they wouldn't get to jazz dance at the Maple Leaf assembly.

I didn't think Mr. Norville would have let them, anyway, since they hadn't even asked him yet, but I kept that thought to myself.

"I wonder if Dustin will be back today," I asked, just sort of thinking out loud.

"Get serious, Carly," Randi said, snorting a laugh. "You honestly think the school authorities are going to let him back in without at least a suspension? They may even expel him. You can't go around hurting people and just, like, get away with it."

"Joey and those guys get away with chasing him around and yanking on his ear nearly every single day, and I'm sure that hurts," I pointed out. "He only ran in front of Alicia once."

"It's not the same thing," Randi said so flatly that I just looked out the bus window and didn't bother to argue.

Dustin didn't come to school that day, which was a good thing, in a way. Just about everybody's parents had been at the town meeting, and most of the kids had gotten a firm warning about the Groats afterward. And in a lot of kids' minds, the danger wasn't just the grown-up Groats but Dustin.

For instance, Leigh Ann was telling anyone who would listen, "Even if Dustin Groat does show up at school, I'm supposed to request a desk in an opposite part of the room. I'm not supposed to be afraid that he'll trip me too or anything; I'm just supposed to stay calm and politely request a different desk."

Adam Gerber said his dad thought Dustin should be frisked. "Or else, those machines they have in the airport? Those gun detectors? We, like, need one here? For just Dustin to go through? Since he's got violent tendencies?"

I knew Adam wouldn't have known what a tendency was, on his own. The other sixth-grade boys loved that gun-detector idea, except they thought it would be more fair if they all got to go through.

"Nobody's even asking any questions!" I whispered to Jasmine as we walked to lunch. "Nobody's wondering *why* Dustin tripped Alicia. And it's not even just tripping Alicia any longer—it's like they're using that as an excuse to also blame him for stuff his family's doing."

"But crime runs in families, Carl," Jasmine said. "Crime families—haven't you heard about those? They've made whole movies about them."

Out in the schoolyard that afternoon, Joey Snyder was standing in the center of a bunch of kids, telling them Dustin would probably be tried by the juvenile authorities, who, he also said, were these really tough guys in black robes that could sentence you to kid jail for years and years, or even for life.

"Can they electrocute you?" Eric Gilman eagerly asked. "Or even, like, hang you?"

"Not usually," Joey answered.

"How about a firing squad?"

"Not usually," Joey repeated.

Something just snapped inside me. I shoved my books into Randi's arms and stormed over to Joey.

"Pardon me," I said, "but I believe in the United States of America you're innocent until proven guilty. So could you please repeat what you told everybody Dustin's crime was that he's maybe getting hanged or going to jail for?"

I had my hands on my hips, but my voice, unfortunately, was stringy-sounding and my knees were even shaking a little, and I could tell people didn't think I looked or sounded as tough and smart as I was wishing I did.

Joey smiled this crooked smile of his and narrowed his eyes at me in this way that means you're just stupid. "Hey, that's for the guys in black robes to find out," he said, shrugging.

Everybody laughed, thinking Joey was cool, and therefore he was right.

Which is why I went to Kosh Woods that night.

I just couldn't live with Joey Snyder getting to decide who was guilty and who was innocent, who was stupid and who was smart, even what was right and what was wrong. It seemed to me all three of those questions, at least as far as Alicia's accident was concerned, could be decided only with information from inside Dustin's own head, and nobody, as far as I could see, was making a move to get it out.

I knew I was disobeying big-time, way worse than I
ever had before in my life. I couldn't let myself even
think about what my parents would say if they found
out. But Mom had told me to put what was really important to me ahead of some other things, hadn't she?
Well, finding Dustin was really important to me, so that
made disobeying her and Daddy just this once one of
those "other things." Really, if you thought about it
right, I would be disobeying her if I obeyed her about
staying out of the woods.

And besides, I kept telling myself, they had absolutely no reason to worry. If there'd been shooting in
Kosh Woods that night, I would definitely have heard it.
I'd checked several times during chores and right after
dinner, and there was only one kind of sound coming
from the woods.

Recorder music. Dustin's music.

I decided if I got caught, I'd better stick with my not-
hearing-guns reason and not mention my obeying-had-
to-take-second-place reason.

I waited, so nervous I felt like I was about to explode,
till everybody was settled in the living room watching a
video together. Then I crept from the brightness of the
kitchen to the sudden total darkness of the porch, clos-
ing the screen door carefully so it wouldn't squeal and
give me away.

The night was misty and overcast. No moon, no stars,
no wind. Breathing fast with excitement and fear, I

jumped the porch stairs and ran through the barnyard, and then on through the soybean field without slowing down.

At the edge of the woods, I stopped to get my breath and to listen. I couldn't hear Dustin playing now, but I couldn't hear guns, either.

There beside the thick trees was when it hit me—I was about to face Dustin and actually talk to him! Not just for thirty seconds, and not even across a page of interview notes. Talk to him, without another human being anywhere nearby! *He might even ask that awful question again.*

No! I ordered myself, pressing my hands over my ears. *Quit thinking!*

I dove into the woods, holding my breath and scrinching shut my eyes, like a kid diving off the high board for the first time. Then I ran on tiptoe, traveling quickly and stealthily toward the only sound—the rippling creek. It was so dark in the woods without the moon. So quiet! Each tree I swerved past seemed to reach out dark, clammy arms to grab me. I knew I should be nearing the bend in the creek where Dustin's tiny cave opening jutted like an eyebrow on the bank, but then again—I could be going an entirely wrong direction.

Something screeched, and I stopped and covered my mouth with both hands. The screech went on and on, an awful high-pitched rip in the silence.

Sharp-edged shadows suddenly grew and tangled over the forest floor, and I looked up and saw the moon sailing free. A few fingers of black trailed across its middle, trying to snatch it back beneath the clouds, but after a few seconds, those fingers lost their grip and things got so bright I blinked.

Huge Chandler's Oak loomed no more than twenty yards to my right, and I saw the twinkle of the creek beyond it. I took a few more stealthy steps, and then I could see the glow of Dustin's lamp in the eye-shaped mouth of his cave.

The awful screeching hadn't let up and was coming from Dustin's direction. Bent so far forward I was nearly crawling, I edged a little closer and saw Dustin's silhouette crouched on the ledge in front of the cave, working at something.

"It's all right now, rest easy, almost done," I heard him whisper, and the screeching softened a bit. Whatever was making that awful sound was right there in Dustin's hands! "Okay, got you untangled, but you best avoid flying through those creek-bank trees. Fishing line's gonna hang you up for good some of these times."

Dustin stood and raised his hands to throw something to the sky. I dropped to my knees as I felt more than saw the dark flutter of bat wings right over my head.

It was now or never. I sprang back up and called out, "Duh . . . Dustin?"

He whirled toward me. I took three quick, clumsy steps out of the brush, into the circle of dim light. "Dustin? It's me, Carly. I came to tell you that you've got to come to school tomorrow. You've got to explain what happened in the gym. They're saying awful things, and only you can stop them."

Dustin stood as frozen as the rock beneath his feet, except that his right hand darted down to clutch something hanging from his belt loop. At first I thought it was a knife, then I recognized the felt case that held his recorder.

I saw him swallow, once. "Don't matter what they say," he called back to me. "I'm done with all that."

"What?"

"I don't care what no one does or says." His voice was toneless as the wind. "Nothing bothers me. It's how a man gets strong and stays strong, like a soldier. I don't let nothing touch me, never."

A bright flash of anger shot through me, giving me nerve I wouldn't otherwise have had.

"I saw your frog house, remember, Dustin? Just now I saw you save the life of that tangled little bat! And Dustin, Nurse Jasper says someone hammered on her office door right after Alicia fell, yelling about an accident in the gym. I think it was you, before you ran on home. I think you were the reason Nurse Jasper got there so fast." My chest was aching so much that I squeezed my arms across it, hard. "You're a kid, not a soldier, Dustin."

I stopped. Some unnatural wind had suddenly come up from out of nowhere, shrieking like a dragon. I covered my ears with my arms and closed my eyes.

"Go back, Carly," Dustin yelled. "It's not good for you nor anyone else to be in the woods tonight."

"I've got one more thing to say, Dustin!" I yelled back. "Our last interview time, you said . . . you said there was something you wanted to ask me, about a sentence from way back in Miss Tyleson's class! If you don't care about anything, why do you still want to know that, Dustin? *Why did you have to turn everything upside down by even bringing it up?* Tell me!"

"Drop, Carly!" Dustin yelled as two helicopters raced right over our heads at treetop level, their searchlights skimming the woods. From where I lay on my stomach, hugging the rough ground, I looked up and saw their propellors cutting the moon to pieces.

Then it was dark again, and against the black sky I noticed the lights of other helicopters over the river bottom, where those two had headed. All those lights seemed like white fingers, fiddling aimlessly with the black sky.

Then suddenly there was a bright-orange flash rising above the river bottom like the biggest fireworks display I'd ever imagined. I screamed and covered my head with my arms as a rumbling boom shook the ground. Too frightened to think, I just huddled there, and when I finally dared to lift my head again and look toward the river bottom, orange smoke boiled in the air like the explosion's shadow. Helicopters darted helter-skelter above it like bugs avoiding a popping campfire.

Far beneath them, fire was spreading along the horizon in both directions.

"Run home!" I heard Dustin scream. "Now!"

I tore my eyes from the fire and jerked my head around to look back at the cave. But though the limestone reflected the orange glow of the sky, both Dustin and his lamp had disappeared as thoroughly as if I'd only imagined them.

I turned and ran then, stumbling through the woods as though the fire were something monstrous rolling up from the ugly river bottom and chasing me.

twenty-three

I didn't slow down at all till I was safely through the soybean field; then I staggered on through the barn-yard, climbed the fence, and dropped in a heap at the edge of our yard. I huddled there, hugging my knees, trying to get my breath back.

"Carl?" Noah ran toward me from the direction of the machine shed. "What's happening, Carly? Are you okay?" He dropped down and grabbed my shoulders.

"Noah, there was an explosion. I think at the Groats'. I was just . . . just out in the soybeans to . . ."

He jerked his head up and looked past me to where the misty sky above the woods was glowing eerily.

"Sure you're okay?" he asked quickly.

I nodded, and he jumped up and ran toward the truck.

"Cover for me, Carl!" he called over his shoulder. "Tell them I had to go to Steve's real quick, for a homework assignment!"

"Noah!" But he was already in the truck, peeling around in the driveway, throwing gravel in all directions.

The price of my silence about Noah driving off to the Groat compound in the middle of an explosion and police raid was for him to tell me every single detail the second he got home.

At about midnight, I heard the swish of him crawling up the vines outside, and I hurried into his room.

"Did they suspect anything?" he asked breathlessly before he was even all the way through the window.

I shook my head. "They went to bed an hour ago."

He took a deep breath and let it out. "Thanks, Carl," he said, stumbling across the room and flopping face forward onto his bed. He toed off one tennis shoe, then the other, then he raised up on his elbows, rubbing his eyes. "The meth lab blew," he whispered. "Unbelievable. There were all these state police out there, 'copters and cars. Most of that wooden part of the fence was blown sky high, and everything's smoke and ashes clear almost to the house. A couple of the Groat men were burned a little, not badly, I don't guess, since there weren't any ambulances out there. They took several of them away in handcuffs while I was over in the trees across the road, watching. I hid the truck nearly a mile away, then snuck close as I could. I couldn't see a lot, but Julie must have known I'd be out there, because she came and found me. She can escape her jailers when all hell is breaking loose easier than she can otherwise. She's okay. She's fine. She's . . . fine."

He collapsed, face into his pillow, arms draped off each side of his bed.

"G'night, Noah," I murmured, flipping his bedspread over him on my way to his door.

Mom was upstairs taking a shower, and Noah, Luke, and I were stacking up the breakfast dishes when Daddy's truck came squealing to a stop right outside the kitchen door the next morning.

Noah and I glanced uneasily at each other just before Daddy stormed through the door, letting it bang on its hinges. I know we were both thinking, *He found out about last night,* only each of us was thinking of a different part of the night.

"They had a stack of these at the elevator this morning," Daddy said gruffly as he threw a copy of the *Kansas City Star* onto the table. "Seems there was a big explosion out at the Groats' last night. Made the big-time city papers."

MAJOR DRUG LAB BLOWS AS STATE POLICE SURROUND COMPOUND, the headline read. Beneath it was a grainy black-and-white picture of a few of the Groats being led away in handcuffs, and a bigger, color picture of bright-orange flames shooting into a black sky.

Noah picked up the paper, first skimming it silently, then reading one section out loud.

"'Sarge Groat, reputed patriarch of the family, was defiant as he was led away in handcuffs. "There's a government conspiracy afoot to destroy the peaceful lives of hardworking citizens!" he exhorted the crowd gathered at the scene. "Civil war is on its way! Those black 'copters are watching not just us but you! Stop the government thugs!"'"

"Whoa," Noah said, dropping the paper to the table.

I picked it up. My eyes were drawn to a word I didn't know. "It says, 'Drug paraphenalia and semiautomatic weapons were confiscated from the compound.' What's a semiautomatic weapon, Daddy?"

"A gun bigger than anyone needs," he told me, dropping into a chair. "You know, when they drove over here a week ago, Sarge was going on about this bunch they call 'patriots' they're linking up with. Said they'd got to know them at gun shows across three or four states. Sarge called them 'men who know a thing or three about protecting their own inalienable rights.'"

Daddy rubbed his forehead. "'Patriots,'" he murmured, spitting the word out like it tasted bad.

Luke's eyes were huge. "Patriots were guys in the Revolutionary War!" he piped up.

"Not this kind of patriot, Lukey," Noah said quietly.

Alicia was back that day, which was great. Not just because she's my friend, but also because she absorbed everybody's attention like a sponge. People didn't even notice I was being quiet. They were too fascinated by Alicia's story about riding in an ambulance, and too busy thinking up elaborate things to write on her cast.

Also there was the huge news of the explosion for everybody to think about. A deep black cloud had blossomed over the river bottom. You could see it clearly in the distance from the right side of the bus. On the ride to school, so many people from the left side of the bus scrunched up with us on the right side that I was afraid we'd tip clear over.

Of course, no one scrunched into our particular seat. Who would have dared crowd Alicia and that huge, white cast?

Dustin wasn't at school, but I hadn't expected him to be.

On the bus going home I was imagining what his day had been like, or trying to, when Randi made a gurgling sound in her throat and stretched luxuriously. "Every single one of our six hundred ninety-seven chickens was awake and squawking all night," she growled. "Must have been all those helicopters."

Her head flopped back against the seat, and a second later she was breathing through her mouth, asleep.

I licked my lips. "Ali, if you're too tired to think about

this, I'll understand. But, can I ask you something about the accident?"

She carefully turned her face toward me, trying not to jerk the sling that held her arm in place. "Sure, Carl."

"I just wondered exactly what you saw when it happened. I mean, did you, for instance, see Dustin's face?"

She shook her head and winced a little. "He was all crouched down. At first I thought he was a basketball. I thought, 'I'm going to trip over that loose basketball if it doesn't stop rolling in this direction.' And then I did trip, and the thing against my legs felt way more hard and solid than a basketball, and as I fell I saw it had been Dustin." She frowned. "I wonder why Dustin tripped me."

Finally! Finally, somebody else had asked why, and it was Dustin's supposed victim. Good old Ali and her logical step-by-step brain.

Right then Randi let out an amazing snore. It felt really good to laugh, though I could tell it made Alicia hurt to do it.

I took my recorder up to the hayloft that night, but once I got there I just sat with it in my lap, looking off to the woods. There was still a purplish plume of smoke above the tree line in the direction of the river bottom.

A few times I heard guns, but not heavy gunfire. I wondered how many of the Groats were left out there, and how many were being held in jail because of the drug lab.

"Knock, knock," Daddy suddenly called out, and I heard his heavy boots coming up the hayloft ladder. "Mind company for a minute? Thought I'd repair that patch where the barn roof leaks."

"I always like your company," I told him truthfully as he hefted himself up through the opening in the floor. He had a few old license plates from the truck under his arm, and a hammer hanging from the loop on his overalls.

I played through a couple of recorder songs while he slid license plates under the rafters in the spot where there had been a dot of sky showing through the tin roof. I waited for him to compliment me, knowing he would before he started hammering.

"How'd I get such a talented daughter?" he asked.

"Oh, Daddy," I mumbled, flustered but pleased.

The hammering took only a couple of minutes, then he came to sit beside me on the floor. "I guess I kind of wanted to talk to you, too, Carl," he told me, "about this morning. I mean, I hope I didn't upset you. I was pretty angry when I heard about that explosion, and especially about that hoard of guns. We all live too close together hereabouts for such nonsense to go on."

"I wasn't upset," I said, swallowing.

"Carly, try to understand what I'm about to say." He opened his pocketknife and began smoothing a ragged place in the old oak floor. "I was angry with the Groats,

164

yes, and I still am. But I guess I'm angrier with myself. All my life I've seen people treat the Groats like they expect the worst from them, and so Sarge and Sol and the rest of them have decided to deliver just that."

He snapped his knife closed and leaned back to pocket it.

"Did I ever tell you that two of Dustin's uncles, Sol and Thomas John, were in my class in school? Yeah, they used to bring a strip of beef jerky apiece every day, just like you were asking me about the other night. They'd eat that and a couple of school milks for lunch, and that'd be all. The cooks used to keep a big basket of apples in the pantry of the cafeteria, and sometimes one of the two, Sol or T.J., would get caught in there, stealing apples. Once or twice, I remember, Sol got paddled so hard for it he couldn't sit the rest of the week."

I cleared my throat. "Dustin could get a free lunch. These days, if your family can't afford lunches you can get a free lunch at school, just for signing up."

Daddy shook his head and laughed, but not a jokey laugh.

"Oh, none of the Groats are about to let Dustin sign up for anything they'd think would have the government nosing in their business, even the tiniest little bit. That'd be the last thing they'd want happening."

He took a breath and whistled it out between his teeth. "I remember back when you were in third grade, Sarge Groat showed up at a school board meeting one night, ranting and raving about the teacher you and Dustin had that year. Turned out she'd tried to get Dustin put into a special reading class. That's what'd set Sarge off. Dustin was having trouble with his work that fall, and your teacher'd asked Sarge to sign a form so she could get him special help with his studies, but instead of signing, Sarge went into a rage about how the government had no business calling his son stupid. Miss Tyleson claimed Sarge had called her more than one time at home, too, threatening her. She finally—"

"Left," I whispered. "She left in the middle of the year." I turned to Daddy. "So, if a kid just decided not to do his schoolwork for some reason, like because he was too strung out or something, the teacher couldn't really help much unless his parents signed a form? Someone could just not learn to read, then. Or learn and then just decide to . . . not do it."

Daddy chuckled, but in a sad way. "Never heard it put like that, but yes, I guess that could happen, all right. I think the school board can set up hearings to get the parents to come around, and can even take it to court. But if parents have decided the school's an enemy, it's all pretty much wasted effort."

"But . . . you'd flunk, wouldn't you? The kid who quit studying wouldn't pass."

"You'd think so. Course, in this state that takes a parent's signature, too. The teacher and school board can try to hold someone back, but in the end if the parents don't go along, it's a nearly impossible thing to do.

And there wouldn't be much point to doing it anyhow if the parents weren't going to get the kid in gear, help him study at home and so forth. As I remember, Sol and T.J. did just enough to barely float along till about junior high, then they both dropped out."

Daddy bent and slowly ran his hand over the gouged place he'd been smoothing in the floor, checking to see that no one would get a splinter from it. "Your great-grandfather built this barn, and it's near as solid as the day he finished it. It's much better to build things solid at the start, Carl, than to keep trying to patch over them later. Patching over a poor job hardly ever seems to hold."

He turned back to me. "Carly, what I was trying to say is, it wouldn't have killed me to put a couple of extra apples in my own lunch sack, way back when I was your age. A little of that kind of thing would have gone a long way."

I licked my lips. "You used to tell me to walk in Dustin's shoes."

He laughed softly. "So, you did remember what your old dad said, after all."

I closed my eyes and took a couple of deep breaths. "You know when I told you that writing is like taking an exciting trip? Well, the problem is, sometimes it takes you on detours to places you don't want to go."

He didn't answer at first, and I wondered if that had made any sense. Then he reached over and squeezed my knee.

"Could be those are the very places you *should* go, though," he said, then stood up to climb back down the ladder.

When he was gone, I just sat there, staring into the night.

twenty-four

On the bus the next morning, I said, "Alicia? Randi?"

I waited till they both were looking at me, then I raised my right pinky finger in the air. "Best-friend top-secret emergency conference, code one."

It was a thing we hadn't done in years, not since we were about nine or so. Would it still work?

They both immediately raised their pinky fingers. "Code-one message received," Randi said solemnly.

"Message received. Awaiting further instructions," Ali said.

Relieved, I leaned close to them and whispered, "The bus gets to the school about twelve minutes before the first bell rings. We're going to sneak into the gym, through the side door. The conference will be held beneath the bleachers."

"But . . ." Randi began.

Frowning, I raised my pinky finger again. Questions aren't allowed when someone calls a code-one conference. And whoever called it got to pick the place, period. Randi nodded and made the sign for zipping shut her mouth.

"It's sticky under here," Randi whispered as her foot came noisily off a dried puddle of something. "There could be spiders, too."

"It kind of reminds me of either a church or a jail," Ali said. "It's so quiet under here. And all these bars of light. Look at our faces."

We looked at one another. We had zebra faces from the sunlight falling between the bleachers.

I led them to the place where I'd read the encyclopedia that day, and after checking for gross stuff on the floor, we sat down cross-legged together there.

For a minute, we just kept looking around us at the bars of light, feeling the mysteriousness of the place.

Then this fluttery feeling started in my chest.

"I called this code-one conference because someone recently asked me an important question, and I . . . I didn't know the answer. I mean, I couldn't answer it. It was about something that happened back when we were just starting third grade, in Miss Tyleson's class. I thought since you guys saw it happen, too, if we talked about it, you could explain . . ." They could explain what? Explain to me that telling Dustin that sentence wrong hadn't been as bad as I was afraid it had? I closed my eyes. "I mean, I just wanted to . . . talk about what happened that day."

But I felt myself chickening out, and I knew I was going to gloss things over, like I had with Luke in the hayloft.

"Euuuwww! What's that?" Randi suddenly squealed, pulling her legs up under her skirt and cringing toward Alicia.

We all three automatically scooted away in the same direction. "What?" Alicia and I demanded together, but I think by then we'd seen it, too. There was something squashed just under the bottom step of the bleachers, about eight feet or so from Randi. It had legs, and eyes.

"Oh, yuck," I whispered, hugging my stomach. "What is it?"

Alicia inched over there to check it out. First she got as close as she could, then, being very careful with her cast, she stuck one leg clear under the little hollow box the bottom bleacher made. With a little sideways gymnastic kick, she scooted the dead thing over closer in front of us.

I gasped. "It's . . . Dustin's frog!"

Alicia swallowed. "I think it matches the foreign matter that was on my knee."

Randi had her face against her knees and didn't say anything.

I saw a popsicle stick lying on the floor and crawled

171

over to get it. I used it to carefully push the squashed frog into the folds of a mustardy napkin.

"It IS the foreign matter you had on your knee," I said to Alicia. "This has to be the 'why,' this little frog. It was Dustin's pet. It must have escaped from his pocket, and all he could think of was chasing it. He didn't see you, Ali. You didn't see him. It was a total accident. After you tripped over Dustin and fell on the frog, it either limped back under here to die or was kicked under here by one of the stampeding kindergarteners."

I looked down at the napkin, but it was blurring. I put my own head on my knees. "Dustin can't even stand to leave a bat tangled up in fishing line. I knew he couldn't hurt a person."

Then no one said anything. The bell rang. No one moved.

Finally, it was Randi who spoke. "Are we all three going to the office to explain this to Ms. Trinny?" she asked.

Ms. Trinny listened as we told her about the frog, but when we finished she said although she appreciated our information it made no difference.

"Girls, I'm afraid Dustin has been taken out of school," she said. "His uncle and sister stopped by my home early this morning to . . . uh . . . inform me of the family's decision. It seems Dustin's father was . . . unavailable to come himself."

In jail, she meant.

"Was it because everybody was blaming him for Alicia tripping?" I asked. "Did they think the school might punish him really hard when he came back or something?"

"Well, that might have been a factor, I guess. But I've been expecting something like this, since a similar thing happened with Dustin's sister." Ms. Trinny leaned forward and covered her eyes with her hands. "In our state, a child can legally be schooled at home if his parents prefer to educate him that way," Ms. Trinny said, as though talking to herself. "And Dustin's parents . . . , um parent, evidently does."

We were surprised at how sad Ms. Trinny looked and sounded.

That morning during one of our work times, Ms. Aspen tiptoed back to Dustin's desk and placed a shoe box on the seat. She bent over and peered into the slot of space where he kept his books and things, wrinkling her nose a little. Then she straightened up.

"Uh, Robert, could you please come back here?" she asked.

She gave Robert the job of taking everything out of Dustin's desk. He was supposed to put Dustin's pencils and stuff in the shoe box and then give Ms. Aspen back the textbooks. .

I folded my arms along the back of my chair, put my chin on them, and watched as Robert pulled out glob after glob of grungy shredded paper.

I was the only person in class, maybe the only person in the world besides Dustin, who knew that was his supply of frog housing.

I walked to the back of the room, pretending I needed to sharpen my pencil. "Robert, I want some of that stuff!" I whispered, and Robert shrugged and threw a glob of that paper at me. I picked it up from the floor and quickly shoved it into my jeans pockets.

Music class that day was a rehearsal in the gym for the Maple Leaf assembly, which was only a few days away.

Josh and Tim showed up for practice without their recorders. As we set up our stands and got organized, most of the boys hung around them like vultures around roadkill, wanting to be close when they got yelled at.

"Boys, please get to your places and quit worrying about the business of your neighbors!" Mr. Norville finally ordered, clapping his hands at them in an exasperated way. "Mrs. Garreuth and Mrs. Simon called me this morning to say there was an unfortunate accident involving both of their sons' instruments. I appreciated their concern and their willingness to promptly pay for replacements. The school has one extra recorder, as it happens, and this afternoon Ms. Trinny and Superintendent Trasker will be going out to the home of a former student to retrieve another. So you see? There's absolutely no problem. The sky is not, I repeat, *not* going to fall!"

This was one of Mr. Norville's jokes, so a few people giggled politely. But my heart had started beating in a dangerous, dark, and angry way that almost scared me.

At lunch we talked about how gross it was that Mrs. Garreuth and Mrs. Simon were always covering for Josh and Tim.

"I bet Mrs. Garreuth said she accidentally ran over those recorders with her station wagon," Randi guessed. "That's what she said that time they tore up their T-ball uniforms, remember?"

"Yeah, and remember that time Mrs. Simon paid Mr. Hankins for that library book she said Josh had read so many times it finally fell apart in his hands? Everybody knew he'd destroyed it throwing it at people during a Cub Scout meeting." Jasmine turned to me. "Remember that, Carly?"

"Yeah," I croaked out. I remembered, all right.

Alicia and Randi and I were planning on burying the frog in Alicia's yard. Earlier, in the rest room, I'd wrapped it mummylike in a thick shroud made of all that shredded paper, and we thought we'd have a simple funeral. Meanwhile, as we rode the bus home, it was carefully balanced on Alicia's cast.

But we ended up changing our plans.

"That thing stinks," Randi moaned, cringing against

the bus window. "You better throw it away, Ali, before your cast gets permanently polluted!"

That scared us, so we opened the window and let the frog in its paper shroud slide into the open air, like they slide dead pirates into the ocean from their pirate ships.

I guess it was littering, but this was an emergency.

twenty-five

Dustin dropped out of school today," I told everybody at supper that night.

Both my parents stopped eating and looked at me. Mom took in a little gasp of air. "Oh, no," she whispered. She looked at Daddy. "He's only Carly's age!"

"His family took him out of school to teach him themselves," I told her.

"Yeah, right," Noah said, "like they'll really do that." I could tell he was thinking of Julie.

Daddy's head drooped, and Mom put her face in her hands. For once, neither of them made any attempt to correct Noah's sarcastic opinion.

My chest had been tight all afternoon, and now my eyes burned, too. "The superintendent and Ms. Trinny took his stuff out to his house this afternoon and picked up his"—I had to swallow several times before I could finish the sentence—"picked up his recorder." *To give it to stupid, careless Josh or Tim.*

"His . . . recorder?" Luke asked in this breathless way.

Yes, Luke, I thought. *Dustin is the Goatboy, Dustin is the mugician, but not any longer.*

I couldn't talk, and I didn't want anyone to see my face, so I turned and pretended to be looking out the window.

Our reflection was sitting there in the window, a glass picture of people who cared about one another. I was made of that care. I was their hopes and dreams for me. How could you grow into something good if nobody was noticing?

"So . . . he doesn't have a wooden flute anymore?" Luke asked.

Poor Luke was growing up.

Suddenly I knew I couldn't even swallow food. "Excuse me," I whispered, and ran for my room.

When I got there I just hugged my arms and paced in circles like a caged animal. After a while I dropped to my knees and dragged out from under my bed the huge old-fashioned dictionary Grandma had given me. I blew the dust off.

"'Nemesis.'" The word was capitalized in this dictionary. "'Greek divinity personifying the righteous anger of the gods,'" I read. "'Child of the goddess Night. Dispenser of retribution, inflexibly severe to the proud and insolent.'"

My hands were shaking as I looked up retribution.

It meant just exactly what I was afraid it would. "'Deserved punishment,'" I read, then put my head in my hands and rocked back and forth there on my knees on the floor.

Why'd you tell me that sentence wrong? Dustin was my Nemesis, all right. My sickening guilt about him was my deserved punishment. Like it said right here in Grandma's huge dictionary, this kind of thing was inflexible. Even mean stuff you did clear back in third grade was bound to catch up with you.

A minute later I heard the door open, then felt Luke's hand like the flutter of tiny bird wings on my shoulder.

"I'm invisible," Luke mentioned softly. As usual, his comment seemed to come totally out of the blue. "I disappear when I have these clothes on, like lions and butterflies. I look like trees in the woods with my magic hat and belt, so I'm invisible."

I squeezed shut my eyes and turned and grabbed him for dear life. He put up with that for a minute or so, then squirmed away and left the room.

I crawled up onto my bed and fell asleep in my clothes. When I woke up several hours later, the full moon was shining so brightly it seemed like afternoon outside, though my digital clock said it was a few minutes past midnight. I stood up and walked to the window, as though pulled there by the moon.

I looked toward Kosh Woods, then opened the window to hear and see better. It was so quiet out there; the whole world seemed to be holding its breath.

Then a strange feeling sailed into me. Not everybody was in the house. Someone was missing—I just knew it.

Noah! I hurried down the hall to check his room, but he was sleeping.

Feeling cold, icy cold, I turned and hurried across the hall to Luke's room.

I recognized instantly that the heap of pillows he'd stuffed under his covers wasn't him. When I threw back his bedspread, a note glowed on one pillow. My hand was shaking so much I could hardly get his lamp turned on.

Dont wory. They wont see me. Im kamuhflajed. Im invisibul.

I barely remember running from his room and stumbling down the stairs, bursting out into the sharp, chilly air, gulping down oxygen and shaking my head—*No! No! No!*

I ran, barefoot, slipping on the dew, batting my hair from my eyes, falling, picking myself up and running, running on through the eerily moonlit barnyard which seemed to go on forever, like a hallway in a nightmare.

The soybeans snatched at my legs, and I looked up at the moon, begging as I ran, *Please! Oh, please, I'll do anything. Anything! Just make him be okay!*

Okay, okay, he'll be okay because there isn't gunfire tonight, can't you hear the nothingness? There isn't gunfire! Calm down, now, calm down. There's no gunfire tonight, and he'll be okay, he'll be okay!

But what woke you up then? Wasn't it the gunfire finally stopping that woke you up? Couldn't that have been it?

"Please!" I was sobbing the word out loud now as I ran. "Please, please, please!" My lungs ached, and my feet were numb. I was more than halfway through the soybeans when I saw the flashing blue lights of the Cooper's Glade ambulance out in the woods, but still I kept telling myself, *It'll be all right, it'll be all right, nothing's going to happen, nothing's happened, nothing, nothing, nothing!*

But I could almost feel that awful child of Night, Nemesis, flying right above me, stretching out dark wings so I couldn't escape her shadow.

And then I saw him, Luke, Prince Lucas the Magnificent, lying on the ground beneath Chandler's Oak, the prince's castle tower. He was a perfect version of himself, except too still and made of silver moonlight.

Four people in white outfits—paramedics—swarmed around him, attaching things to him, to his chest and head. I knew one of them—her name was Becky and she'd taught my Brownie troop first aid. I heard myself making a sharp, strangled sound, like an animal being tortured, and Becky whirled around and saw me.

"Carly," she said. She rushed to me and grabbed my arms. "Run home and tell your parents to meet us at the emergency room at the Regional Health Center in St. Joe. Carly?"

Things got fuzzy at the edges. Becky gave me one hard shake. "Carly! Don't faint on me, Carly. Your brother's been shot in the heel. It doesn't look too bad, but he's also got a head wound from falling from the tree, and that worries us more. I need you to hold yourself together and get your parents to the hospital! Are you with me, Carly? Go! Go *now!*"

She ran back to help the others. They had Luke on this shiny, wheeled bed. They were lifting him into the ambulance. Where were they taking my brother?

"Carly, snap out of it and go tell your parents!" Becky yelled to me as she jumped into the ambulance behind Luke, then slammed shut the double doors. The ambulance squealed away along the rough truck trail through the woods, throwing blue light on everything it passed.

"Okay," I whispered, then moved like a sleepwalker to the spot where Luke had been lying. "Okay, Becky," I repeated. "Okay."

Something white glowed at my feet. I picked it up.

It was Luke's little whistle, the one Grandpa had carved for him out of three pieces of straight white elm.

Luke had climbed the castle tower so he could search through the woods for the Goatboy. I was shaking so hard I didn't know if I could stay on my feet, but I guess I did, and somehow I ran home like Becky had ordered me to, clutching in my numb hands the little whistle Luke had been bringing to Dustin.

twenty-six

In the hospital, I put my brain on automatic and told Luke nonstop stories about kids from the rings of Jupiter with eyes in their elbows, and about circus animals that took over the world and taught humans tricks. I told him stories of kingdoms and lands beneath the ocean, and glittering jewel mines where elves and land whales worked together in the center of the earth; I pretended it was just those bedtime-story days again, for both our sakes.

Mom and Daddy made me go back to school the fourth day after his fall, so I could tell him stories only afternoons and evenings. They read to him the rest of the time, and Noah gave him play-by-plays of every baseball game he'd ever seen.

The bullet wound in his heel was already almost mended after a week, but he wouldn't wake up from the concussion he'd gotten when he'd fallen from high Chandler's Oak.

"Talk to him, the more the better," Dr. Heathly told us. "If he does wake up, hearing is the first sense he'll probably regain."

"Not *if*—*when,*" Noah said firmly for us all.

The eighth day after Luke's fall, Ms. Aspen gave us an essay assignment at school, to replace the interview project.

"I've given this lots of hard consideration, class," she told us. "I believe we've learned our lesson and thought enough about cheating, and now we need to emphasize the positive."

I wasn't so sure anybody had thought about their part in rigging the interview project for even a single second, but I didn't, of course, correct her.

"You're to write a personal-experience essay entitled 'I Was Proud of Myself When . . .' The essays will be read aloud in class next week, and we'll vote for our newspaper editor afterward."

Eric Gilman shot up his hand. "When what, Ms. Aspen?"

I tuned out and opened my notebook. At the top of a clean sheet of paper, I wrote down the words Luke had put his faith in—truth and freedom. I drew clouds surrounding each of them, and while I was doodling around the edges of "truth," it occurred to me that maybe God was like George Washington to the umpth degree, and maybe he was waiting for me to come clean before he granted my prayers.

I fingered my writer's bump, then turned to a new page and quickly wrote the title of my essay on the top line: *The Wrong Sentence*.

I wrote and rewrote the entire thing that night in the hospital, ran it by Luke, then volunteered to read it aloud right before the end of class the next day. Why wait? The quicker God heard it, the better.

I was nervous standing there in front of everybody, but not embarrassed nervous. Sad nervous, afraid I might look at Dustin's empty desk at the wrong time, while I was still trying to read.

"My essay on a time when I was proud of myself is called 'The Wrong Sentence,'" I began, then cleared my throat. I glanced over the top of my paper and saw Randi and Ali looking at me. Ali smiled, biting her lip, and Randi raised her pinky finger.

I took a deep breath and started.

"'I was proud of myself in third grade because I was the best reader.'"

I glanced up to see everyone's reaction—I'd been afraid they'd think that was bragging, even though back in third grade it had been pretty obvious. No one was rolling their eyes or anything now, so they all must have remembered.

"'I was proud that I could read without stopping

to sound out words, if all the words were one or two syllables. I could even read one four-syllable word—"homogenized"—from the milk carton. I couldn't really see how anybody could be a better reader than I was—I mean, except for maybe adding more syllables.

"'At home, I assumed everyone was standing around, waiting for me to read to them. When my little brother toddled by, I would sometimes tackle him and sit on him and read to him until he screamed for our mother. I read to my cat, Twinkletoes, for hours each night, and she purred, which I took as a sign she was impressed.'"

Everyone laughed a little, and I started the second page.

"'Dustin Groat, on the other hand, had been a pretty good reader in second grade, but all of a sudden he wouldn't bother to keep track of where we were in the reading book. Or in any subject, for that matter. When Miss Tyleson would start calling on people to read aloud or do arithmetic problems on the board or something, I would wave my hand wildly in the air, bouncing in my chair. But Dustin Groat would actually sink his head down into his shirt collar like a turtle, because he had no idea where we were in the lesson.'"

I heard some people shuffling a little, and I glanced up to see them looking expectantly at Ms. Aspen. They were probably surprised that I could talk about someone's bad behavior without the teacher stopping me. I looked at Ms. Aspen too.

"Go on, Carly," she said, so I cleared my throat and went on to page three.

"'I became so disgusted with how Dustin was not paying attention in class and acting weird on the playground that I wanted my brother to either beat him up or have him arrested. So I kept trying to get across to my family how truly awful he was.

"'"Dustin Groat kicks gravel at the climbing bars," I kept telling my parents. "And he head butts people going up the slide. And he says cuss words!"

"'One night when I was going on and on like that, Daddy said, "Carly, maybe you shouldn't be thinking so much about Dustin Groat. I mean, maybe you should try a little harder to walk in his shoes."

"'I felt flustered and confused. I couldn't stand to be criticized by Daddy about anything, but there was no way I was going to stick my feet into Dustin Groat's sweaty, muddy, old, beat-up shoes!' "

I paused, expecting laughter here. But when I glanced up, everyone was just looking at me, wide-eyed.

I turned to page four.

"'So I went out onto the porch, where Mom was sitting on the porch swing and folding clean clothes.

"'"This Dustin Groat," I told her, "well, sometimes at recess he spits, like he's been chewing tobacco. I think he *does* chew tobacco. At least, he smells like it."

"'"I thought you said he smelled like mud," Mom said, smiling a one-side-of-her-mouth kind of smile.

"'I spotted Luke, then, playing in the sandbox under

the big sycamore tree in the side yard. More and more that fall when I was eight and he was two, Luke seemed to be the only person in the whole family who paid close attention to everything I said. I ran over and dropped to my knees in the sand beside him.

"'"Guess what? Dustin Groat smells like tobacco juice and mud *both!*" I whispered into his ear.

"'Luke laughed and laughed.'"

I paused, swallowing hard a few times. I heard a few sniffles across the room, too. Everybody was really, really worried about Luke.

I turned to page five.

"'And then, in November, Miss Tyleson moved Dustin to my table. We sat four people to a table in third grade, and she moved us every few weeks.

"'"Dustin Groat writes his name on the table in *spit!*" I told my family, sure that finally they would take the awfulness of Dustin Groat seriously. "I could get germs. Awful germs!"

"'Mom and Daddy exchanged a look across the spaghetti bowl that night. Then Mom said, "Carly, surely Miss Tyleson has things under control. But . . . well, to be on the safe side, you stay in your own place and don't . . . change spots. I mean, isn't that what you're supposed to do anyway, sit in the same place every day without moving to anyone else's part of the table?"

"'"He spits on the whole table," I said slowly and dramatically. "Just to be mean," I added.

"'I didn't think it was really a lie, because I knew in my heart Dustin would have spit on the whole table if it had occurred to him.

"'Still, when Luke chose that second to throw his spoon onto my plate, I nearly jumped out of my skin. I jerked my head toward him, and he began slapping the noodles around on his tray and laughing at me like I'd been caught in the act of something.'"

Some people had laughed when I was talking about all that spit, but it got really quiet when I switched back to Luke again.

I put that page, page five, behind the others, and then just stood there for a few seconds before I started on the last page. I couldn't look up to meet anyone's eyes, but I could feel their eyes on me, all forty-two of them—forty-four, counting Ms. Aspen's.

"'By then, November, I could tell Miss Tyleson had almost given up on Dustin taking part in class. I mean, she'd gradually quit calling on him, though she called on everybody else.

"'But then out of the blue one day, she ignored the fact that hands were waving all around the room and that Dustin Groat was trying to disappear down into his shirt as usual, and she did call on him to read the next sentence in our reading book.

"'Dustin gulped and shot me a hot-eyed sideways look from under his eyebrows. And then . . .'"

I stopped and took a deep breath, not sure I could do this.

"'And then, Dustin leaned over to me and whispered, "What sentence are we at?"

"'I had never been so shocked in my life, not even when I was five and first found out we were going to get Luke. I wasn't shocked that he'd cheat or anything like that. I was shocked that I actually had power over rude, kicking Dustin Groat. I assumed people like that always had all the power.

"'My heart raced and my neck felt like it was burning.'"

As I read, my heart raced and my neck burned.

"'"Come over here and get this cat if you want to give it a bike ride," I whispered to Dustin, ducking behind my own third-grade reading book so Miss Tyleson couldn't see.

"'Dustin Groat sat up very straight and spoke loudly: "Come over here and get this cat if you want to give it a bike ride."

"'Everybody exploded in laughter, because I'd made that sentence up out of thin air. The *right* sentence read, "Some of their baseball bats have bright red letters on each side." Dustin melted down into his seat, exactly like the Wicked Witch in *The Wizard of Oz* had melted when she was hit with water.

"'And everyone in class, all of you, only you were in third grade and not sixth, everyone laughed and laughed, and I was proud because everyone was laughing about something funny Ed done.

"'But now I wish God had a huge pink eraser and

that he erased each day when the sun set to make way for tomorrow. But I know the past is still here because I melted Dustin with one simple sentence that day, and he stayed melted. You saw him back there in the corner of our classroom, still melted after three complete years.'"

That was the end of what I'd written. I put page six behind the others and took a half step toward Ms. Aspen's desk, then turned back to the class.

"And the awful thing is, why'd he ask me for help in the first place that day, instead of just shaking his head and refusing to read like he usually did? I've asked myself that a kajillion times, and there's only one possible answer. He must have wanted to start being one of us again. He'd had a horrible thing happen that had made him into a wild animal that fall, but now he was ready to work his way back to being part of our class! He trusted me that day, and I could easily have helped him. But instead of trying to walk in his shoes, I thought to myself, 'This is only Dustin.' So I humiliated him instead."

My hands had blotchy red dots all over them as I put the six pages on the edge of Ms. Aspen's desk. Without looking to the left or right, I took my seat and put my head on my desk. I curled my left arm around to cover my face.

A few seconds later, something touched me. I assumed, of course, it was God, out to get me. But it was Alicia and Randi, patting my back.

twenty~seven

But deep inside this dark place, if you only knew,
Are wings—tangled, torn, but yearning for flight.

It was the last line of *Earbug,* and it came to me as I made my way through the frozen soybean stalks on a cold December afternoon eight weeks after I gave my report in class. I went to the woods that day to leave the little elm-wood whistle Grandpa had made for Luke on the tiny ledge of rock beneath the mouth of Dustin's cave.

I wouldn't have gone into Kosh Woods if there'd been any chance at all that there was still gunfire there. I would have found another way to get the whistle to Dustin, because I know how much our parents can stand and that would have been too much.

But ever since three of Dustin's uncles were questioned about Luke's accident and then put under arrest, the woods have been as still as a storybook forest when the book is closed. Or as when a curse descends and the entire kingdom falls into an enchanted sleep.

Noah says the Groats know that if any of them are caught with guns in the woods before the trial, things will go much worse for them. That doesn't mean they won't be back after the trial.

The tree branches were coated with a thin shimmer of the first ice of winter the afternoon I left the whistle. Icicles hung from the ledge of rock like frozen tears falling from a giant's dark eye.

Afterward, I went home to wait, but I didn't hear Dustin. And each night last week when I came home from the hospital, I went to the hayloft to check. But there was never music coming from Kosh Woods.

Randi and Ali went to the hospital with me last Friday and came home with me afterward. They've been to see Luke lots of times, of course, but this was the first time we'd been together, the three of us alone, for weeks. Randi suddenly has a boyfriend who's taking all her time—a guy from the junior high basketball team. And Ali has been all wrapped up in helping coach the gymnastics team, since her arm has been broken and she hasn't been able to compete. She's even gone to a couple of movie parties with some of those kids.

I'm busy myself—with Luke, of course, and also I was

elected editor of the class paper. I even have a staff of volunteers. Who knew Krista and this girl named Angela were interested in writing, just like me?

Things change. Old things end, and new things start. When you stop and think about it, Randi and Ali and I don't have all that much in common any longer. I mean, now it doesn't seem to be enough that we just live down the road from one another.

Still, it makes me kind of sad. We went up to the hayloft last Friday night to watch the mid-December meteor shower—the "star dancing," as Luke has always called it. Alicia kept absentmindedly rubbing her arm as we sat watching the sky. Her cast had been off for only a week.

"Does your wrist hurt?" Randi finally asked her.

Alicia crinkled her nose. "No, but it just sort of feels like something now."

I guess lots of stuff is like that. You don't notice it till it breaks, then it feels like something all the time.

Finally, just the other night, six nights after I'd left the whistle, I heard music coming from Kosh Woods.

It was different than the recorder music had been, more filled with wind, but just as beautiful.

I jumped to my feet and stumbled down the hayloft ladder.

The moon was very bright, and the stars were still dancing against the black winter sky. The moonlight was reflected in the ice along each soybean stalk, so the field was filled with little sticks of light. I ran through the frozen stalks, and they crackled against the legs of my jeans.

At the edge of the quiet woods I stopped, my heart racing, wondering what I was going to say or do. My breath froze and glittered around me, then drifted away into the night. I walked slowly toward the bend in the creek.

I know Dustin sensed me approaching, because the music stopped. The crunch of my feet through the skim of ice on the forest floor was loud and sharp as I walked that last eight or ten steps past Chandler's Oak and on to the tiny cave.

Dustin was crouched on the ledge of rock, in the same position as when I'd first seen him there, except without his frog to admire his playing. He was lit from behind by a lamp just inside the cramped cave opening, like before. It struck me again that he seemed almost carved from the same stone that the cave had been carved from. The whistle looked so natural in his hands that it seemed like part of the same stone statue.

To my surprise, I suddenly wasn't afraid, or even nervous.

He was looking at me when I stepped into the small golden circle the lamplight made on the icy forest floor.

"I wanted to tell you that my brother is going to be okay," I said. "He's awake and getting back to normal. It was you who called 911 that night, wasn't it? You might have saved his life."

"Will you thank your little brother for the flute?" Dustin said quietly. "Never nobody gave me such a gift before."

I nodded. "He loves to hear you play. You're good."

He ducked his head, then lifted the little flute and played a couple lines of melody, ending in a trill.

"Could . . . could you come play for Luke in the hospital? We're supposed to be talking to him and stuff like that. Your music would be even better."

He dropped his eyes and shook his head. "They wouldn't have me there."

It took me a while to figure out he meant my parents.

"They don't blame you," I whispered. "They're trying not to blame . . . anybody. But they'd never blame you."

Then neither of us knew what to say next. I wanted to ask if his arm was okay, and if his ear was okay. I wanted to ask if he was okay. But I couldn't bring myself to.

"I'm sorry about your frog," I finally pushed out.

And then it was quiet again.

Dustin fingered the flute but didn't blow. The dark, half-frozen creek crackled along, and behind us Chandler's Oak seemed to be in a deep winter sleep.

I knew what had to happen next. If these old woods were under a frozen curse, there was only one thing that could lift it.

"I did tell you that sentence wrong," I whispered. "I made you hurt worse when you were hurting so much already. I didn't even have a reason. All I can say is, I'm sorry."

A mourning dove called out deeper in the woods, and another one answered, even farther away, as though spreading news through the darkness.

I took a deep breath for courage, then plunged in.

"Dustin, I'm editor of the class paper now," I said in a rush. "It takes lots of time, and with Luke and all I only took the job for one reason. I took it so I could . . . could write my first feature article about you. It was my interview report, really. I wrote about your pocket frog and how sad it was that it got squished. I wrote about your tunnel and about how you play recorder so well. People didn't roll their eyes about it, Dustin. They were fascinated—really! Mr. Norville told me he thinks you could possibly be playing these hard patterns called modal scales. Even Joey Snyder was interested, at least in the stuff about that stiff blood on the Civil War uniform your family owns."

Dustin jerked up his eyes to glance at me, then he swallowed and looked down again. Was he mad? But I'd come this far and had to finish.

"My parents went with me to talk to Ms. Trinny, Dustin. She thinks if you and your sister went to the school board and made a formal request for you to go back to school—both of you—well, she thinks they might be able to make it happen. Ms. Trinny told us that when you home-school somebody, you have to keep a journal of hours you spend on it and what you teach your kid, and if Family Services gets a complaint that you're not actually *doing* that, they have the right to come in and ask to see the journal. And if your parents don't have a journal or refuse to show it to them, the authorities have the legal right to put you back in school. So, if your dad hasn't really been teaching you . . ."

I held my breath, crossing my fingers inside my jacket pockets so hard my knuckles ached. But Dustin stared down at the whistle in his hands and didn't move a muscle.

"Dustin? See, nobody in town can figure out a way to get behind those walls at your compound. My parents, for instance, want to help, but you and Julie are the only ones who can tell anyone what goes on back there. Things . . . things would be different if you came back to school, Dustin. They would. People are sorry. I promise. We can go to the school board anytime . . . you say. My parents will pick you up."

But all of my wishing and promising couldn't turn stone to flesh and blood. Dustin didn't move.

"If you're worried about, you know, your reading and stuff like that, well, I'll help you catch up. It would be the least I could do after, you know. What I did. In Miss Tyleson's class." Using more courage than I dreamed I had, I stared at him, hard, till I finally knew he could feel me. "Please, Dustin," I added, my voice cracking, "give me another chance. My parents will take you to meet with the school board . . . anytime."

But he still didn't answer, and finally I turned to walk away. Why should I have even hoped he'd want anything to do with any plan of mine, after what I'd done to him? Nothing could change yesterday.

"Tomorrow?" Dustin suddenly whispered, so softly that at first I thought his voice was just the wind, which was moving carefully through the brittle trees now, bending them toward us expectantly.

author's note

School law varies from state to state. Within these pages, I've tried to accurately portray current Missouri legislation regulating home schooling, grade retention, and the sometimes tricky balance of parental responsibility and administrative policy. I've interviewed many administrators and teachers in an effort to be accurate, and have, indeed, served as a school board member myself. Law in this area is currently changing quickly. What remains constant is the untiring drive toward excellence of Missouri's educators.